The Echo Glass

Heather Morrall

TeenFiction

a division of Rubery Press

TF

Published by
TeenFiction in association with Rubery Press
UK
ruberypress@aol.com
First published by Lulu 2006.

ISBN-13: 978 0 9554252 0 2
ISBN-10: 0 9554252 0 4

For Abigail Chaffey and Elaine Green.

Part One

Angel

1

Corisande comes running up to me at lunchtime. "How dare you?" she screams.

I stare at her. Since starting Year 8 Thursdays never seem to go right for me.

"Pardon?" I say trying to keep calm.

"You can't keep anything to yourself. You told Beth about my beads. Don't ever spread lies about me."

I lean on my left leg, putting all my weight onto it and bobbing to the side. It's what I always do when I'm angry.

"I didn't mean to tell her, but I was laughing and she kept nagging me and..."

"I don't want to hear this," she says putting her hands over her ears in a childish way as she walks out of the room.

There is something inside me. I'd never felt it before this year at school, and so I call it my alien feeling. It feels like something is growing stronger maybe like roots sprouting fast inside me and spreading.

The real trouble had started earlier in the day at break time ...

We all know the school uniform policy. It's

drummed into us everyday. Today Corisande wants to ignore this. She wears beads (gold and silver sparkling ones) over her navy jumper and they dangle down for everyone to see. She's proud of them and all the girls think she looks so cool.

How can I be surprised when a teacher sees them? The Monster, big and fat, marches up to us holding out her huge hand.

"Shame," Cori mutters to me as I hold my breath trying to keep a giggle from escaping out of my control.

The teacher looms down. Her mouth opens and she roars ferociously, "You won't get this back for two months."

"No way!" Cori says.

The Monster glares at her, "The school uniform policy is clear for everyone. You chose to break it. I shall be sending a letter to your parents and you'll stay behind for an after school detention." The words stop for a brief second before she continues. "Rule-breaking is taken very seriously in this school."

I feel my hands quivering and my legs shaking. I am standing so close to The Monster.

She marches off to find someone else to catch.

"Oh no, Jas," Cori says putting her hands over her embarrassed face. "My Mum will kill me."

"Really?" I say trying to be sympathetic. "Can't you just tell her it was a mistake and the teacher's got it in for you?"

"How embarrassing! Was anyone round listening? Imagine people seeing!" she looks around her to see who is there.

"No, no there was no one here. No one saw

anything." I link my arm through hers to comfort her.

"Oh man!" she says starting to laugh. "Imagine sitting in detention with HER! Did you smell her smelly breath?"

"It stank of coffee."

We both laugh.

She clings onto my arm tighter, "Jas, don't ever tell anyone about this."

"I won't."

"Promise?"

"Yes. I'm not going to tell anyone."

I like people trusting me with their secrets. I feel kind of important.

"I only wore the beads because I thought everyone in the class would like them. I was going to take them off when I got to my lessons."

I nod, pretending to understand.

Mrs Corcorran, head of our year, walks towards us. Cori looks at me and then whispers, "She won't know about my beads will she?"

"I doubt it," I say reassuringly.

"Corisande, could you just run down to the paper room and order me some paper for my office this afternoon?"

Cori looks eager and nods. I can see the relief in her face for not being found out.

"Oh, you're such an angel," she says as she begins to walk away in her busy shoe clicking walk.

"See ya in a bit then," Cori says to me. Her face is still wrinkled with smiles and I can't help but smile with her.

She walks up the corridor and I walk in the opposite direction. We have Geography in different sets so we won't see each other until lunchtime.

Beth is waiting for me outside the classroom. I hate sitting on my own in lessons so I'm lucky to have Beth to sit with. Beth's best friend, Ruth, is in Cori's set so it's as if we swap best friends just for the hour.

I try to stop laughing when I see Beth but my face just keeps crumpling into lines of smiles. Cori's embarrassed face won't leave my mind no matter how hard I try.

"What's so funny?" she asks, her blue eyes bulging out of her head with curiosity.

"Nothing, Beth. Honest."

"Please tell me," her small voice almost as delicate as porcelain.

"I can't, I promised Cori I wouldn't," I say still trying to stifle the giggles that keep escaping.

Her eyes seem as huge as the fruit bowl at home.

"You've got to promise that you'll never tell anyone," I say leaning towards her and speaking confidentially.

She nods.

"Well, it's just that Cori's had her beads confiscated and it was really funny. I promised I wouldn't tell anyone because she's so embarrassed."

"She had them confiscated?" She laughs with disbelief. "She was showing off about those beads this morning saying no one would dare confiscate them off her."

"Really? She just told me that she was going to take them off when she got to class to make sure they weren't confiscated!"

We laugh.

"Promise you won't tell anyone?" I say, feeling

guilty for telling her. I wish I could have stopped laughing and then I wouldn't have had to tell her.

"Of course I won't tell anyone."

We walk to our desks and unpack our books from our bags. I sit down and wonder if the hour will go quickly today.

Cori comes running up to me at lunchtime. "How dare you?" she screams.

And now Ione, Cori's sister and all her friends in Year 10, have been told of what I did to Corisande. They surround me, asking me to justify myself, but when I open my mouth to try nobody listens. Sounds stutter from my lips, but the minute they hear anything their mouths become smiling bananas and their eyes seem to be full of hate for me.

Cori's so popular with everyone. But we just seem to be arguing all the time nowadays. It's almost like she doesn't want to be my best friend anymore. She has so many friends and they all cut me dead for the rest of the day. I see them talking in whispers and pointing at me.

Their words echo in the windowed school, bouncing against the delicate glass. They sound like the clappers of a bell, ringing constantly.

I no longer watch T.V. when I come home from school. I spend hours in my bedroom just thinking. I can't help but go over the day in my mind, re-living each fragment.

I remember when we first started Garret Bell. We'd only been there for about a month but Cori and I were already best friends. She was the perfect friend I'd been hoping for all of my life ...

"I don't cook much at home," I say to Cori as we

stand at the tables in the H.E rooms and stir our mixtures round the bowl.

"My Mum always lets me and Ione cook. We used to make cakes every week – spreading that icing on thickly!" she says.

"Hmm, yummy," I say thinking about tasting a delicious, freshly baked cake. "I love it when they're still warm."

"Oh definitely. Just not toooo hot or else you burn your tongue!" she says, laughing.

I pour my mixture into the baking tin, poke the prongs of my fork into the top so that it will rise properly in the oven.

The heat from the oven throws itself at my face and I shuffle back a little until it's a bit more bearable.

I slam the door shut, stand up, rub my hands together and smile.

The smell of cakes and shortbread cooking fill the classroom.

Cori and I sit together and smile.

"We've only been here a month," she says, "and I feel like I've known you forever!"

"Oh, I know! It's brilliant! I've had best friends before, but not like you. You're just brill."

"Aww, that's so sweet. And I've never had a best friend like you before either. Give me a hug."

She reaches over to me, her arms stretching over my shoulders and gently holding me. I smell the shampoo in her clean hair. I feel safe with her; as if I can tell her anything and she'll never laugh at me.

We let go of each other. "You are still coming to mine tonight aren't you?"

"Yup."

"Good. We can eat our shortbread together!"

With the towel wrapped around my hand I open the oven door and lift out the baking tray. A perfect looking tray of shortbread stares back at me.

The teacher walks towards me.

"That looks good," she says as she puts the knife in to see if it's cooked all the way through.

I feel a warm feeling seep through me and I feel proud.

"I'll just look at yours in a minute Corisande."

Cori lifts hers out and then looks at me. "Jas," she says quietly. "Mine hasn't got the fork marks in. Mine looks a bit brown round the edges." She places it on the table and looks up at me worriedly. "What am I going to do?"

I look over my shoulder to make sure the teacher isn't looking and then pick up my fork. "It'll be ok," I say handing her the fork. "Just put the fork marks in now and then she won't know that you didn't do it before it went into the oven."

She hurriedly puts the fork marks in; rows of four holes.

"That looks nice, Corisande," the teacher says as she looks down at it. "I'll give you both an A for your shortbread."

"See!" I whisper to Cori, "She didn't notice!"

We walk home with our brown H.E baskets dangling from our arms. Our steps are slow. Cori has shoes that click on the pavement. Mine don't make any sound. I'll have to remember to find shoes that click when I get new ones next year.

Cori looks at me and smiles, "Let's eat our shortbread now."

"What, outside while we're walking? In this cold air?"

"Yeah, why not? It'll warm us up. Feel that," she says making me touch the bottom of the basket. "It's still warm from when we took it out the oven."

We giggle as we uncover our baskets and break crumbs off.

"Oh yum, yum," she says. "Now I bet you can't even remember why you wanted to wait until we got home to eat this."

I laugh. "Actually, I can. I didn't want to share any with Ione."

We burst into huge roars of laughter.

"No, no, that's what I should be saying! I hate sharing with my sister! This way we get to be selfish and eat it all ourselves! Besides she must have done this in first year too."

"Oh, my stomach feels huge but this just tastes far too good."

"Let's eat the whole thing."

We sit together on the wall outside someone's house, shovelling in the shortbread and laughing at the same time.

"I'm winning," I say. "I'm going to finish before you."

"Oh, not fair! You can't win." A crumb flies out of her mouth, "Oh no, look I missed that bit. It escaped!" And we laugh harder.

"All gone," I say holding my stomach. "I don't know how we're going to walk the rest of the way home, I feel so sick."

"Ugh, me too. We'll just have to. No way can I miss *Neighbours* we'll just have to make it. Besides Mum'll probably be calling the police by now."

We cling onto each other for balance and a long, sluggish walk home.

16

"You promise you'll always tell me everything?" Cori says to me.

"Of course. I have no secrets from you. I never will."

"Friends forever then?"

"Friends Forever!"

And we laugh all the way home ...

I miss those happy days we had together. The thoughts constantly play in my head, reminding me of what I have lost, what we had when we were friends. I miss her so much when we're not together.

I get a piece of paper out and pretend to write my diary on it. I'll let Cori see it tomorrow. It's not to hurt her. It's just that I need her to know how upset I get when we're not friends. I admit I do make stupid mistakes every now and again and I shouldn't have told Beth.

I sit at my desk in my bedroom and fiddle with my fountain pen. Then I put it down and write the note in biro. I hate biro.

Dear Diary,

I've lost the key to my diary, you see, but I really need to write to somebody. This note NOBODY must read.

I have lost my best friend. She's always talking about me behind my back. She fell out with me today because she thought I was talking about her behind HER back, but she wouldn't let me explain what happened. I didn't mean to break her secret and it was an honest mistake. I'm not perfect.

We broke friends earlier this week and she said some very hurtful things, shouted out private things in the corridor for anyone to hear (it was about Nathan, the guy who lives on my road).

I don't know if I ever want to forgive her. If we were ever friends again she'd have to be very, VERY sorry for the things she's been saying about me.

I don't know why I care so much. I know I shouldn't but I do. I would really want to be her friend again but I'm not sure if we should be best friends.

We used to say, 'Forever Friends' or 'one, two, three, sorry!' and we'd be friends again. This time it's her turn to say sorry.

I hear the key in the front door and mum comes in. She calls up the stairs that she's home. I don't respond.

I look at the piece of paper that I've written my pretend diary entry on and then look at my real diary.

It's quite a nice notebook. It's a hardback book with a woman who has long blonde hair and a pink flowing dress. She's holding flowers in a field. I often think of her as my friend and hope that she can understand me. I started to write my diary when I began Year 7 at Garret Bell. Cori had given it to me as a present.

I can't help wondering what has made things change so much since I started senior school. Why is it that this alien feeling has taken root inside me?

I close my eyes and listen to the words of my CD which is playing. I keep playing sad songs all the time nowadays. Since I can't describe this alien feeling I'll let the singers sing about their pain instead.

2

At the beginning of Tutorial I put my books and pencil case onto the desk. Out falls the pretend diary that I'd written for Cori the night before. It flies onto the table and straight in front of Cori. I couldn't have planned it better if I'd tried.

"Oh, sorry," I say, snatching it up quickly but I lose grip of it and let it fly further away from me. Cori picks it up and opens it.

"What's this?" she asks.

"Please don't read it. I lost the key to my diary and I needed to write in it so I wrote the entry on a piece of paper." I don't think I want her to read it now.

I watch her read.

"You make it sound as if it's all my fault."

"No," I say. She is a blinding angel and my anger melts in her saintly light. "I don't mean to. I was just upset. I want to be your friend."

"And I want to be yours."

"Then where's the problem?" I ask.

"There shouldn't be one."

"I've got an idea to stop these stupid arguments," I say.

I open my Nike bag and pull out the Forever

Friends paper that I keep. I start to write a note. Then I fold it over and give it to Cori. "If we ever fall out you must show me this note and we must instantly forgive each other. It's not good the way we keep fighting this way."

"Ok," she says putting the note in her bag. "Can I come and sit with you again?"

"Yep."

She smiles her banana smile and her soft voice rings in my ears with the doubt that hasn't quite left.

Being with her reminds me of when we were best friends in First year. Even then I knew she was hurting me. I remember all the times she made me feel special and wanted. It was those times that made me want her friendship.

My diary details all the events and feelings that she has caused:

Wednesday 5th November, Year 7.
Dear Diary,

My best friend is very pretty. She has a foreign look about her: big lips, dark brown, shiny hair and sparkling eyes. She hates the slight moustache that she wants to bleach and is sensitive about. Her eyebrows meet in the middle and she talks endlessly about this. Her eyebrows are her only imperfection. She's gorgeous. She knows it and so does everyone else.

She told me today that, "Eyebrows that meet in the middle are meant to show that you're bad tempered." But she said her Mum won't let her pluck them until she's eighteen.

We're eleven (though I'm twelve very, very soon) and we're pretty grown-up now.

I told her, "I wouldn't worry about it, you're not

20

bad-tempered" and that she should "set an example for all those people with eye-brows which meet in the middle."

Personally, I can't see the point in all that pain just to get rid of a few hairs.

Besides, I want people to know she's bad-tempered. (Does that make me a bad person?)

"Hardly anyone has naturally black hair and blue eyes," she said today for the first time ever. "You're so pretty."

I felt so embarrassed! Mum said that she sounds gushy and I think she's right.

But I do wish that I could say the right things to people like she can. Her confident smile hides all her faults. Her calm, gentle voice consoles the girls in need. Her morning hello won't be sufficient, she has to hug everyone but smiles archly at me (can you tell I've been using my thesaurus? Archly sounds more grown-up that slyly).

Everyone loves her. No one loves me.

Love,

Jas xxx

I put my diary down and think about Cori's looks. It's strange how she appears to be so saintly when she's clearly nothing like an angel. But there is a distinct glow that must radiate from within. Sort of like a majestic feeling when you stand before her. Everyone loves her and wants to be her friend. That must be what it is. It's everyone else's opinion of her. How can anyone not be an angel when she's so perfect?

The Main Toilets at school are disgusting. For some reason Cori always insists on going to them. They've been painted in pink that has chipped in most places and the mirrors have red lipstick kisses on them.

Cori has her hands under the dryer. I've got wet hands and so I touch her face. We always do this. It's a silly tradition. We just giggle.

She doesn't giggle.

"Don't do that, Stupid," she says staring at me for a minute.

"I'm sorry. It was meant to be a joke."

"'I'm sorry,'" she mimics, "'It was meant to be a joke.' At least I don't have a posh accent like you. You're such a snob. And at least I don't look like you."

She starts to laugh while looking at me from head to toe.

"And look at the way you stand," she's muttering the words now as if she's scared someone will hear her. With one last look she leaves.

When the door closes behind her I hear thrilled screaming from some girls that must have been standing outside.

"Oh Cori! We were wondering where you were. We were so wanting to see those new earrings."

"Oh those," I hear her say. "They're ok, I guess."

I imagine her shrugging her shoulders, secretly pleased with the attention. Her brown hair will shimmer and shine as it always does.

I feel like a fool.

I run to a cubicle and cram myself inside it, crouching on the floor. All the echoey voices begin to dribble away from the toilets and a silence fills the space.

I get my diary from my bag, unzipping it

slowly just in case there is anyone still here who is listening to me or in case Cori decides to come back with her fan club.

Tuesday 15th February, Year 8.
Dear Diary
Enough is enough. I don't want to be her friend anymore. She hurts me too much. I can't cope with this yo-yo friendship. There's such a strange feeling inside me. It's like the Alien is being watered with April showers because it grows so strong so quickly.

Cori just seems to want to hurt me. Maybe her aim is to wreck me.

I'm a loser! Look at me sitting here on the floor in the girls' toilets. LOSER!

After the afternoon registration bell has rung I leave the toilets. I walk slowly along the corridors hoping to delay the inevitable. I open the classroom door but hardly anyone is there. I sit at my desk and wait for them to all come back.

The door flings open and Cori runs up to me out of breath and flashing a huge smile.

I don't smile. I will stick to my vow and will not be her friend. I have to protect myself no matter how lonely I might feel in future.

"I just wanted to show you this," she says.

It is the note I had written her on the Forever Friends paper.

"You can rip it up for all I care," I say through clenched teeth. But I don't mean it. I stare in front of me trying to show that she can't hurt me anymore.

The form tutor walks in and Cori glides back to her new seat at the far side of the classroom.

I watch her as she sits at the red table. She turns her head towards me and smiles. A flash of lightning strikes from somewhere deep inside and her eyes seem to glow a deep red colour. Her fingers grip the note tightly and then she tears it to shreds.

The fragments of paper with blue ink over them are spewed over the red tabletop. She leans forward and blows elegantly at them. Some seem to rise slightly from the surface and move along the sea of red as if travelling on waves. The others sink on an undulating wave.

She lifts her head and continues to smile. It's all over and she turns away. Satisfied.

The bits of paper lie where they've drifted. They look as if they've been meticulously torn into a work of art. But I know it is Cori's intention to declare each fragment worthless. I hope that my name has been torn up so that no one can identify the pieces with me. Cori will be thinking the opposite.

"Corisande, would you hand these worksheets out to the class? Thanks," the form tutor says. He looks at her, his favourite, A-grade student.

Cori stands up and collects the papers from his desk.

Everyone loves her. The teachers always give her tasks to do because she's clever and does as she's told and they seem to like the banana smile she smiles to them. It's only me that knows what she's really like. I long for our confidential conversations that we used to have, sharing our deepest darkest secrets, and all the laughs that we had in between all the bad arguments. But now it's only ever the arguments that we have.

I wait until I'm home before I cry. The roots from the Alien are digging into me and causing so much pain. It seems to grow and thrive on all the hurtful words that are said to me.

I used to think Cori was human and had faults like everyone else. Thinking that made it all seem ok and that it was worth making friends again because this time would be different. But her faults don't seem like anyone else's. I keep seeing little bits of her that remind me of evil. It's like a lovely green apple that you bite into. Once you've bitten it you realise it's all brown and disgusting inside. But by then the rotten bit is in your mouth and you can taste it.

3

"I'm too ill to go to school today," I say to Mum.

"I'm sure you'll feel better once you're there," she says.

"I'm ill, Mum. I can't." I feel the tears trickling behind my eyes.

She can't force me to go and so I don't go. Days have gone by since Cori tore up the Forever Friends note. I can't seem to shift the evil image out of my head of her ripping it to shreds. But knowing that Cori is at school and probably hanging around with Ruth and Beth makes me sad even though I'm not her friend. All I want is to feel a part of things and to belong.

"This is to do with Corisande, isn't it?" Mum finally says.

"No. I just don't feel well"

"So are you two friends?"

"Well, not really. But that's nothing to do with it."

"I'm going to phone and speak to her mum because all this arguing isn't helping anyone."

I wish I'd never told her about not being friends last year. Just because she knows how often we fell out she's getting silly about it.

"Oh Mum! Please don't. It's got nothing to do

with her."

"Will you stop whining, Jasmine?"

I know it's not a question by her tone. I scrunch my face up when she's not looking. She hasn't listened to a word I've said.

"When you go back to school I want you to go and talk to a teacher about this."
I agree with her just to make her stop.

When *Neighbours* is on I can hear Mum speaking on the phone in the hall. I sit in the living room with my ear to the door.

I can only hear muffled words. I push my ear more firmly to the door.

"I'm just concerned," I hear her say. What's she concerned about? "Worried about how it's affecting Jasmine... Could you maybe speak to Corisande about it?"

She's talking to Cori's Mum.

"Bye." And then I hear the receiver smack against the plastic telephone base.

My heart sinks. There is no way I can go to school after this. I will be the victim of abuse. Why can't she stay out of it?

Darkness slowly suffocates the light from the sun. It comes too quickly. I climb into bed trying to think of more ways to get time off school. I close my eyes and see darkness and blankness. There are no more excuses. But now that Mum has spoken to Cori's mum all hell will break loose.

The cold morning wakes me up. I hear Mum turning the taps on in the bathroom. I have no excuse. I just have to say I'm still ill.

"You can't keep having all this time off," she says.

I don't say anything.

She sighs loudly. "Ok, well I have today off work anyway. So I'll be around."

I go into the living room and turn on the TV. There is nothing else to do but watch daytime TV.

"I've made an appointment at the doctor's," Mum says as she walks into the living room holding a pile of washing. "You've had a week off school and we need to make sure there is nothing seriously wrong."

"Fine," I say.

I walk up the stairs to stay out of her way.

I close my bedroom door and sink onto my bed where my diary lies. I want this alien feeling inside me to die. Its roots seem to just keep on growing and becoming more entrenched in me.

The diary looks inviting and so I begin to write:

Wednesday 13th March, Year 8.
Dear Diary,

I'm not happy. I can't even pretend anymore. It feels like life is falling to pieces around me.

Mum is taking me to the doctors next week. She's only doing it to persecute me and to make me pay because I haven't been to school in ages.

What's the point in seeing the doctor? He can't do anything. I'm not ill in a way that anyone can see. Am I even ill? I'm in a lot of pain but doctors can't give painkillers to a pain that can't be seen. It's going to be a complete waste of time.

I just don't know what I'm going to do. Help me?

Love,
Jas xxx

I flick through the pages and stop at the first non school uniform day we had. I close my eyes and wonder if that was when I first realised I didn't fit in with everyone else at school ...

We used to have toy-days in junior school at the end of term. I used to take my Barbie dolls in with their Porsche. It used to be such fun.

But now at secondary school these are the days that we wear our own clothes for half a day.

Before the day even arrives there is so much chatter about it. We all seem to look forward to it and there are waves of whispering and planning while everybody decides what they'll wear.

I choose my clothes carefully. People can be cruel. I may only be twelve years old but I know that people can be especially cruel when it comes to clothes. And I don't like being laughed at.

I choose a pink cotton top, and my knee-length skirt in a softer pink. I wear my black, canvas shoes with white ankle-socks. Just before I leave the house I notice a silver locket on my dressing table. I fasten it around my neck and watch it drop and rest just past my collarbones.

I smile. I think I look quite nice.

"You look lovely," Mum says. But the nerves don't die.

She takes a picture of me with my new camera. She bought it for me at the weekend because my old camera broke and she knows I want to be a professional photographer. But it's not one of those zoom lens digital cameras that I really want because they cost so much money.

The camera flashes and clicks and then she hands it to me.

"Take it with you to school. You can take

loads of pictures of your friends."

I feel embarrassed taking a camera with me. But I'd like pictures of them so that I can glue them into my diary and remember them forever.

"Jasmine!" Cori shouts as I walk into the classroom. "What do you think of my clothes?"

She's wearing her blue Morgan trousers that cling flatteringly to her legs. Her satin black top shimmers against the light and her long brown hair hangs loosely around her shoulders.

"You look lovely," I say. She always looks lovely. Her brown hair, thick and long, always shines and glows. And her skin is flawless, never a spot in sight.

We go out into the corridor by the lockers and I take my camera out. "Smile!"

She doesn't smile. She presses her lips tightly together and pushes them out into a pout. She puts her arm behind her head and her other hand on her hip. "I'm a model," she says as she raises her head to the ceiling.

I laugh.

She snatches the camera out of my hands and takes a picture of me standing in front of the windows that wall the corridors.

She smiles innocently, "Come on let's go and join the others."

"Hey Jas, is that your camera?" Ruth says. Even though she's best friends with Beth I get the feeling Beth would rather be Cori's best friend.

I nod.

"Oh go on take a picture of us all. We know you'll always take good photos of us!" She turns to Cori, and adds, "though since it's not even a digital camera it'd take a miracle to get a good picture!" And they chuckle.

30

The group hunch together so that they'll all fit into the picture.

The camera flashes and the film rolls on. I've nearly used up a whole film already.

"Let's see what everyone's wearing," says Ruth as she throws her blonde hair behind her shoulders.

We form a circle with the other girls. Ruth goes round each one of us and tells us what she likes about our clothes.

"Corisande, you look so perfect. You should be a model," she says. Cori smiles, and briefly glances over at me. Then she listens to more compliments from the group.

"Yeah Cori, you always look great. That shade of lipstick looks fab on you."

I look at her lipstick and notice how big her lips are. I wish I had big lips.

"Yeah very sexy!" one girl says.

Everyone shrieks with laughter and Cori does a little wriggle with her hips and pouts some more.

"Jasmine," Ruth says. She looks me up and down. I hold my breath and wait for the verdict.

Everyone is looking at me, pricing me up. How much am I worth? "I like your locket," she says slyly and swiftly moves on to the girl next to me.

I hear someone whisper, "She's better taking the photos than being in them!" And they giggle.

Cori laughs in my ear and I pretend I'm not affected by her words.

I half hope that someone else will receive the same verdict. I look at Ruth who is in charge of the class. Who will tell her if she looks ok? Her blonde hair is too long and rests in straggles

31

down her back. But I know it would be cruel to tell her that...

I continue fluttering through the pages of my diary. The words reach up to me with a strange despondency.

What on earth will I tell the doctor when I see him?

4

The doctor can't find anything wrong. I'm a fake and they've sussed me out.

"Your dad," he says softly.

"Oh, I'm fine about my dad," I say.

"Are you sure?"

I nod.

"You don't feel you need to talk about it?"

I shake my head.

He sighs.

"What about school? Is there anything happening in school that's making you worry?"

I shake my head.

"Right. We'll make an appointment with the nurse to do a blood test. I don't think you're anaemic but it's best just to check. Don't worry about it."

Mum drives silently to the next appointment. I sit in the back watching the houses spin by. The lull of the road calms me.

The nurse rolls up my sleeve and ties something around my arm. I turn away. I've never had my blood taken before but there's no way that I want to see the blood in the tube. I feel the prick as it goes in and then it stays there.

"Is it coming out the right colour?" I say looking at the door.

"Well," she says, "it's blue so I guess that's normal!" She laughs.

I laugh.

The results come back even before the bruise on my arm has healed.

There's nothing wrong.

I'm disappointed. It's as if this is confirmation that there is nothing inside me hurting. It's all made up. I'm going mad!

It's been three weeks since I've spoken to Cori. She could have forgotten the whole episode of my mum phoning by now. Maybe there won't be any rumours echoing when I go back. But I know that Cori will be acting like she's best friends with Beth by now.

The first thing I notice when I walk into the form room is that Cori's back in the seat next to mine. I stand by the door before walking all the way to my seat. Her angelic look is back on her face. She doesn't have blonde hair and yet each strand of hair reflects the classroom lights, bouncing sparks around the room.

She seems to be talking to me.

"Have you been in your locker today?" her big, faintly-coloured lips parting to allow the words to squeeze through.

"Might have," I say, reluctant to give any more information than that. I sense there is something going on, a conspiracy against me.

The electric bell rings through the hollow cup of glass. All the girls troop out for first period. I lag behind.

When Cori has left I open my locker. There is

nothing there except a white piece of scrap paper. I look again in case there's something I've missed.

Nothing.

I look at the paper. My fingers begin to shake and my heart beats fast. I feel sick. The pain is racing around my body entering every limb and weakening it.

Dear Headache,

I heard what happened on the phone the other day and we think it's scum, just like you. Me and my gang don't want to hang around with scum.

It's written in crooked letters so that I can't recognise the handwriting. This must be deliberate because it is also signed with four rows of dots. But it's so obvious who it's from. Why else would Cori be so eager for me to open my locker? She just couldn't wait for me to discover the note as soon as possible. Is Beth involved in this too?

"Did you write the note, Cori?" I say it as nicely as possible because I don't want another falling out.

"What note?" she says without any sense of surprise.

I show it to her.

"No I didn't. How could you accuse me of that?"

"Sorry, I just don't know who it's from." I still think it's from her but decide not push it so soon after my mysterious illness. Besides, I could be wrong. I don't have any evidence.

"Just chill. It's probably nothing," she says.

I just want a quiet life. I'm not even going to pretend to care anymore. But since coming back after being away for so long I just feel like an outsider.

Not only that, but something changes. It's so sudden it's like a bus has charged down the road and hit me straight in the face.

I have a plan.

I could lose weight.

"I'm not overweight," is my first thought.

That's not the point, I say, thinking about it again. *You want this horrible feeling to go away and it will if you listen to me.*

I can't see what I have to lose by listening. I look in the mirror at my stomach. "Maybe you're right," I say, thinking about what it would involve.

That's better. Everything will be fine when you weigh six stone seven pounds. I promise. You're only a stone away and as you're only five feet three inches you can afford to lose every pound.

It's as if there is another person in me. The pain has become a person and is talking to me. More to the point I'm not on my own anymore. *I can cause hurt inside you. But I can also make everything ok too. You've felt what I can do. Now you need to listen to what I say and then you'll be ok. LOSE WEIGHT!*

"I'll try to lose weight. My legs do look very fat," I say looking at them. I can always stop if it doesn't work.

Write 'I am fat' a hundred times every night. Because you've got a bigger problem than just fat legs! You need that drummed into you.

So I write with my blue biro, which I hate. I finish my one hundred lines and file them not having the nerve to throw them away as if I'd be

36

throwing a part of myself away.

My faithful friend, my diary awaits for its news update and so I fill it up with my newly found hope.

Thursday 20th March, Year 8.
Dear Diary,

Suddenly I have opened a door to a new world, a magic world. There's hope in sight and I can reach it if I just try hard enough. I just have to lose weight!

If I have strict rules and think about nothing but food, calories and exercise then I won't have time to think about the hurt I can feel inside me. The Alien did hurt me, but now I realise it was hurting me because I didn't know that I could listen to it. And now I can do as It says! And It is also my friend. It looks out for me.

Think of how happy I will be to be able to succeed at something!

I wonder why no one else has thought of this! It's pure genius and I'm the one who's stumbled upon it. It's just my secret – me and my little world together.

I'm so happy, for the first time in a very long time!!

Nothing can touch me now.
Love,
Jas xxx

I worry a little to begin with. I've heard of something called anorexia. But I don't think I really care. Nobody else does. Besides anorexia is something that skinny people have.

The New World is all encompassing consisting

of food diaries and weigh-ins. The one diary lists the food that I am allowed to eat for the next day. The other is a diary to keep track of all my sins and failures.

There are rules: I must NEVER eat ice-cream again. It will make me fat overnight.

I must weigh myself EVERY morning and night.

I draw my magic number on sheets of white A4 paper. I colour them neatly in purple and draw flowers intertwining the purple numbers.

This is my master plan. And all I need is determination.

There are negative words constantly spilling through my mind, "Oh, I shouldn't have eaten that. I can't eat as much tomorrow."

You'd better not because I'll make you feel horrible.

Even though the words from the Alien are negative they offer me guidance and hope.

"I'm trying," I say, "but it's hard."

I know but it'll be so much better when you're thin.

The Alien, that constantly grows stronger, is a part of me. I can't even tell when It's speaking or when I am.

At school Cori keeps saying, "You don't need to diet." I know her too well. I can see her angel image and I don't believe a word she says.

She starts to laugh, "Hey," she says to some girls in our form. "You know Jas is on a diet? Well, ignore her because she's doing it for attention." She looks at me and laughs. They're all laughing at me.

"Beth," I shout as I see her walking down the corridor. "Let me come with you."

"Shut-up," she says. "You only go on about diets and that's because you want people to say you're thin. Well we're not interested."

"I don't want people to say I'm thin. I'm just talking about my diet because it interests me." It's clear she's siding with Cori on this.

"Well, it bores us."

"Fine, I won't talk to you about it. Don't worry."

But food is priority. Nobody is letting me talk about the one thing that matters to me.

So much time is spent everyday wondering what to eat and whether a Jaffa Cake is permitted when I get home from school. What should I eat if I can't have a Jaffa cake? Is there such a thing as a safe food?

Cori's theory of the attention seeking behaviour is being shaken as if it were the clapper in a bell. It rings in my ears in shrill sounds.

"Jas," Cori says to me one morning. "I'm stressed out. I think my mum and dad are splitting up. Dad had a nervous breakdown and Mum can't cope now."

"Oh, I'm sorry," I say because I don't know what a nervous breakdown is. I daren't tell her that though.

I think back to when I used to go to her house quite a lot and what her dad was like. I can't ever remember speaking to him.

"Well, try to forget about your family and we'll have a good time together. We could take photos after school, if you like."

"What of?"

"I don't know but we've got all afternoon to

think about it. I should think there's something somewhere that's interesting!"

She looks bored and throws herself off the table and leaves the room.

Monday 28th March, Year 8.
Dear Diary,

Cori's dad is having a nervous-breakdown. Do you know what that is? I wish there was someone I could ask so I could find out. I can't ask Mum because then she'll want to know why and I don't want to tell her. The dictionary was no big help either. I'd use the internet at school but I don't want anyone to see what I'm looking at.

I'm prepared to be her friend for now. I know it's rough when you're alone and things are so tough. But I AM concentrating on my diet. I'm cutting down on the fat and the calories. It's just so hard, ya know?

Today I ate:
Breakfast: a bowl of Co-co Pops.
Break: NOTHING (yay!).
Lunch: one sandwich and an apple.
Dinner: baked potato with salad and chicken.

My weight this morning was still a lot. I was a terrible seven stone three pounds. But I'm getting there. It just feels so great to be losing weight, almost like I'm having my own private party!
Love,
Jas xxx

5

I stop listening in lessons and start to dream. I stare while something creeps around my mind as if it were an old, cautious cat exploring new territory. I'm running out of class from a teacher who has been nasty to me. I run to the stairs and then I fall. My body crumbles to the floor and drags itself down each concrete step until it reaches the foot of the stairs. There I lie, blood on my face, limbs tangled like a ball of wool the cat has played with. Faces peer down at me.

"Call an ambulance!" someone screams. "Jasmine, open your eyes. Are you ok?" Someone's fingers press the side of my throat.

"Her heart's beating," someone says relieved. Their arms gently lift my head and they put it on their lap.

"Please open your eyes." The blood still drips from a wound on my head but someone's firm hand holds something soft to my face. I'm scared, but I'm safe in their hands and in their control.

The paramedics arrive. Their voices secure and safe. I lie still and confident that they will help me as they take me to the ambulance and settle me comfortably inside. I won't open my eyes. I feel that as long as I keep them closed I can stay in the safe haven. A teacher comes with me, I don't know which one, just one who holds my hand. Then the ambulance drives away from school.

Then what? The dream ends. I wake up in the classroom where it isn't safe. I start the dream again, focusing more intently on the injuries, of the fall down the stairs. Sometimes I dream that I die.

"Jas?"

"Hmm?" Cori's face glows as if it were the sun burning in front of my eyes.

"Are you all right?"

"Yep."

"You looked like you were in a trance or something."

"No, I was just thinking."

"About Nathan, I bet."

"No I wasn't," I say angrily.

"How could you fancy him?"

"He's nice."

"But he's so ugly." She laughs.

"Looks aren't everything, ya know."

"But his spots! Imagine kissing him! No, don't. I feel sick."

"Leave him alone." I'm talking in that whining voice Mum always tells me not to do.

"Why, have you slept with him?"

"Get lost." I roll my eyes and say, "what-EVER."

"Do you remember that letter you got in March?" she says, changing the subject.

"What letter?"

"The 'Dear Headache' note."

"Yeah." I immediately forget about Nathan and wonder if I'm going to get a confession.

"Beth wrote it."

"Bethany?" I look at her with surprise. Can she really be telling me the truth?

"She told me she'd told you. She has, hasn't she?"

"No."

"Oh, no. You won't tell her will you? Please don't tell her."

I look at her for a minute caught in her bewitching trance.

"Corisande, I love your shoes!" a girl from behind calls out. I hope she's saved me from making any unwanted promises.

"Promise?" hisses Cori into my ear.

"My mum told me to never make a promise," I whisper back. I pick up my Parker fountain pen and start to fill out the questionnaire that sits on my desk.

"Bitch," she says in my ear.

The lesson ends and I pack my bag, throwing in the books and papers not caring how crushed they will get. I sling the bag over my shoulder and run out of the room and away from Cori's words that she throws. The door closes and I run down the corridor and to the dinner queue.

"Beth, wait!" I shout and I join the queue next to her.

"Why are you going into the canteen when you're sandwiches?" she asks.

"I'm breaking my diet. I'm going to have chips." I smile at her and she returns it. I link my arm through hers.

"Jas, I've got to tell you something," Beth says looking uneasy. "Me and Ruth have fallen out," she stops and looks at the floor briefly. Then she adds, "For good. This time it's for good."

"Oh no," I say.

"Cori said that I can hang around with you two now. I hope that's ok?"

"Of course that's ok!" I say, thinking that it'll be good to have an extra friend. Maybe things will be ok now if Beth is with us. Cori might even stop falling out with me all the time.

But I've got to find out who really wrote that note. I can't stop thinking about it since Cori accused Beth. I have no idea what to believe anymore.

"Well, I've got to ask you something," I say as the queue sluggishly moves to the counter.

"Leave your bags in the hall, Ladies," the dinner lady says loudly in her screeching voice which punctures through the noise of the girls queuing in the hall. I put my bag next to Bethany's on the wooden boards that stretch along the hall and we continue with the sporadic movements of the queue until we reach the canteen.

"What is it?"

"Remember that note I got in my locker?"

She nods.

"Cori told me who wrote it." I stop in case she wants to jump in and save me from my accusation. She doesn't. "She told me you wrote it."

Her delicate, thin lips move apart and her china words fall out. "Cori's lying. You know what she's like. I didn't write it. It was when you were away for ages, she asked me to get involved but I wouldn't."

I watch her pull her tray in front of the dinner lady's spoon. Food falls onto it and I mechanically move mine in her shadow, as if she were leaving a trail behind for me to follow.

The golden, crisp chips fall onto my plate. I stare at them and walk along pushing my plate on the counter. I pick up the salt, shake the snow onto my plate, replace it and then stare at the puddings.

"I love chocolate slab cake," I say. She turns around and smiles her doll face smile. This is the only good thing about canteen meals. I put the chocolate slab cake onto my plate.

We find seats by the window. I watch her pick up her knife and fork and cut the food to smaller bits until it will easily poke onto each prong. Then neatly enclosing her lips around the mound of food she slides the fork out between her lips and chews the food.

I pick up my fork and prod my chips. "I never know when Cori's my friend or not. Sometimes I don't even know what I've done to her to make her fall out with me."

"I know. She's like that with everyone. Try not to worry about it."

"I can't help it. She turns everyone against me. You've seen what she's like. I just don't know what to do."

"Don't do anything. Talk to me, we're always friends."

She's right, we are friends. But Cori was my best friend before Beth came along and so my loyalties must always be with Cori.

I push a few chips into my mouth and chew them slowly. I look up suddenly to say something but her white, porcelain face looks as if it would shatter. I leave my chips and turn to my chocolate slab cake. I pick it up and take a bite. It doesn't taste as nice as I'd remembered;

nothing tastes nice. I drop it on my plate and Beth looks up suddenly.

"You all right?"

"No. I don't like it. Food's lost its taste. I shouldn't be eating it anyway." I look out of the window and watch the children play.

"Ever wonder what it'll be like in Year 10?" she asks.

"I can't imagine what it'd be like." I laugh. "Year 8 is hard enough, just imagine, soon it'll be September and we'll be in Year 9!"

"I know, it's scary."

"Sometimes," I say leaning towards her. "I have a nightmare about being anorexic."

She looks at me. "Eat your dinner then."

"I will. But I remember talking about it with Cori and we didn't know what it was. You know what we said? We decided that if we were ever anorexic then it would be good because it meant we were thin!" I stop and stare at the food on my plate.

"My mum knew this anorexic girl. She starved herself down to four stones and she had to go into hospital."

"Is she all right now?"

"Not really, they say she might die."

"Do you know her?"

"No. I've never even met her. She just worked at my mum's place. Mum didn't really know her that well."

The words falter from our mouths and silence seeps between us. The canteen noises creep around our ears but we can't hear them.

"Perhaps I should tell you," she says, lowering her bulging eyes to the table. "I did have something to do with that note. Cori dictated it to me. I'm sorry Jas, but she made me."

"She didn't make you," I hiss, jumping up from my chair. "You chose to do what she said." I throw my fork onto my plate which makes a plastic crash. I leave the table where I had sat so comfortably with the sun melting the uneasiness that had existed inside me.

I walk back to the form room, hunger vanishes and anger takes its place. Having proof that Cori really was behind the note makes me even more angry than I'd been when I'd only suspected her.

Cori sits eating her lunch in the form room. I walk over to her and sit down silently.

"What's wrong with you?" she asks.

"Nothing."

She chews the white bread and her angel shine radiates around her face and spreads to my vocal chords.

"Actually," I say wondering if I should confront her about the note. "I was wondering how your dad was." It's safer to ignore the note.

"He's okay, I guess. I think he's getting better." She looks out of the window, and I see her cheeks burn with embarrassment of the subject. "How's your dad?"

"My dad?" I ask.

"Yeah."

"You know he's dead."

"But I asked my mum about that and she said he didn't die."

"Your mum doesn't know everything, you know." I jump up in a hurry but reluctant to break friends I say, "What room you in for French?"

"Forty-six."

"I'll walk you down there." She links her arm through mine and we walk out of the classroom.

"So what's happening at home? You haven't said anything recently," I say.

"Oh! Well, Ione's got a boyfriend!"

"Really?"

She nods eagerly.

"Wow. What's he like?"

"He's not too bad. She'd kill me if she knew I was telling you though!"

"So is it serious?"

"Not yet, but, hey, you never know!" She smiles and I feel her angel glow seep through to me. I'm glad I'm her friend. What would I do without her?

6

"Beth," I say. We've calmed down after I'd stormed out of the canteen. "I'm sick of Cori. I want her to know what it feels like to have friends turning against you all the time."

Since having it confirmed that Cori really was behind the note in my locker I just keep thinking that I need to teach her a lesson. I want the Alien to take root in her too. Just for a while anyway. Until the three of us can all be friends again I'll just hang around with Beth. I quite like the fact that someone else can understand what Cori's like now.

Beth looks at me. I've caught her attention and her bulging blue eyes stare intently at me.

"What did you have in mind?" her voice has substance, no longer weak.

"I don't have anything in mind. I wish I did. But if I think of something would you help me?"

"Hmm. Probably."

"Okay, I'll think of something tonight and we'll talk about it tomorrow."

Thursday 17th June, Year 8.
Dear Diary,
I've thought about revenge for Cori. But how do

I do it? There's only writing a note to let her 'accidentally' see but I've already done that. Besides, by trying to tell her how much she hurts me only makes me weaker against the power she seems to have over me. I've got to make sure I'm safe from her angel influence so that I don't start believing what she says.

There's only one thing for it, I'll have to break one of her secrets. She'd be so angry that she wouldn't be able to shine and smile her big-lipped banana smile. Her face would no longer be serene.

That's what I'll do! I'll tell Beth about Ione's new boyfriend!

Love,

Jas xxx

The sun has slithered away from the sky and to the other side of the world. I open the top drawer in my dressing table and find the old make-up Mum had given me. The blue eye-shadow, black mascara and red lipstick. I dip my finger in the blue eye-shadow and smear it around my left eye then I close it and cover the lid to make sure it looks convincing. The mascara makes the finishing touches by giving a tinge of black. The mirror reveals a painful bruise when I turn on the light so that I can see. The lipstick is ideal for blood and I make a trail of red from my lip to my chin. Then I finish the picture by putting a smudge of red on my forehead.

I am the victim of violence. I smile to myself. The injuries reassure me and I feel a safe warm feeling. The Alien approves.

I lie down on the floor, facing the ceiling which has lots of white blobs and streaks over it. They remind me of the diagrams in the science books at school of eggs and sperm. Perhaps one day I will be able to tell Cori this and we can laugh about it.

I close my eyes and dream my dream of falling down the stairs. It is in dull colours but the intensity of the feelings are increased. I am running so fast but the feeling inside is so powerful that the fall downstairs doesn't bring relief from the Alien. But there are kind words being used around me and to me. It soothes me a little.

I open my eyes but the horrible feeling fills me again so I close them and try not to open them again. I want to make this real. I want to kill the Alien inside.

You're forgetting I'm here for your own good, the Alien says. *The reason you feel horrible is because you're fat. It's perfectly simple. Lose weight and you'll feel fine.*

And I know It's right. But it doesn't make the pain any easier to deal with.

"Did you think of anything then?" Beth asks the next day, her voice seems strangely frightened.

"Yep. I did." I smile smugly to myself, relishing my master plan before it's brought out for someone to hear. But I feel uneasy. I'd dreamt about the beads incident last night. I hadn't meant to tell Beth that Cori's necklace had been confiscated. But I did break her secret and so Cori does know what it feels like to have secrets broken.

"Well, it's just that I was thinking we should spread one of her secrets around like she's done to me."

Beth nods, "Those secrets she spread about

you fancying Nathan?"

"So embarrassing," I say. "The thing is I'm not so sure we should now." I feel myself thinking very hard. "I don't think it'll work," I say.

Beth shakes her head.

"The beads," I whisper.

"I was just thinking about that. Look how she reacted to that."

"We'll have to think of something else," I say wanting to find something that will make Cori realise the hurt she causes.

"Is there anything else we can do though?"

I shrug. It feels hopeless. All I want is for us all to be friends. Since Beth no longer has a best friend maybe all three of us can be best friends. But it seems impossible to have that if Cori doesn't know how she hurts us with her nastiness.

People have left the form room while we talk. Only a few girls sit on their desks, kicking their legs underneath it and laughing with their friends. Beth's hair looks more golden than usual while the sun shines over it.

The door violently flies open and Cori walks in. She silently walks over to the window and pushes it open. For a moment she stares down the three storey building, glass all the way down. Her wild eyes dart about the room as she walks over to me and Beth. Her hands snatch at Beth's bag.

Beth opens her mouth to protest but a flicker of fear wavers in her eyes and she closes her mouth.

I secretly hope that Cori will do something drastic so that everyone will see how terrible she really is. I feel disappointed that there are so few girls in the form room to witness this. But at least Beth will understand what she's really like so that I won't be alone anymore.

She flings the bag out of the open window. It falls down the side of the glass as if plummeting through the water of a silent ocean, spreading ripples of silence to the surrounding people.

I try to look horrified, I really do. But I can feel a smile trying to sneak onto my face like it did when she'd had her beads confiscated. I try to control the muscles that persist in forcing my mouth to turn upwards.

I watch. Cori's brown hair is tangled and her eyebrows are closely joined together. But she still looks beautiful. She turns to me, her face is serene. I feel the smile that had wanted to creep onto my face disappear with the fear of seeing her calm, shining face.

"That's Beth's bag!" I shatter the small ripples of silence.

"Beth's?"

"Yes. Wasn't that your bag?" I look at Bethany and see her eyes are as watery as the ocean her bag has fallen into.

She nods.

Cori sees the watery look, "I'm so sorry," she says. She walks over to her and reaches her arm across her shoulders. "I'm sorry, I really am. I thought it was Ione's. We fell out, you see, and she told me she'd left her bag up here and sent me up to get it for her."

I watch Beth's china face crumple slightly under her kind words, but really she cries from the relief that Cori is still her friend. I go over to the open window and peer out of it. There on the concrete floor is the bag lying lame. The contents are strewn out as if it were the blood bleeding from a body.

"I'll get your bag then, shall I?" I ask.

"Oh, would you Jasmine? You're so kind." Cori barely lifts her eyes to say the words.

I smile a contrived smile because Cori dismisses me so abruptly. I go to fetch the bag obediently like a dog. Nobody seems to have seen Cori's true colours like I'd hoped they would. They seem oblivious. No matter what Cori does she seems to have fooled everyone into believing she can do no wrong.

The contents of the bag lie on the floor and I crouch down to pick them up and put them inside. It seems impossible for us all to be friends, but I wish we could.

I can hear the Alien persistently telling me to stop talking to them and to hurt Cori. At the same time the roots surge out and hurt me more just because It agrees with all of her comments when they're aimed at me. I deserve them. That's all there is to it. No room for argument.

When I return to the classroom Cori has left and Beth sits alone.

"Here's your bag."

"Thanks," she says taking it from me. "Is there a reason why Cori is so short tempered at the moment?"

"I don't know why. Maybe because she has problems at home. Her dad's had a nervous breakdown."

"Oh, well that explains it." Her words are china again.

I don't want Beth to hate Cori because I know how nice she can be when she's our friend. We like Cori. She's a laugh. Without Cori, Beth and I can't even be friends with each other because Cori would never let us get away with that. It's either the three of us together or none of us.

I lean towards Beth and say in my gossiping voice, "Ione's got a boyfriend."

I hope she'll feel interested and forget the hurt she feels from Cori.

"Really?"

I smile and say, "We'd better get to class, you know."

"Yeah. Thanks for getting my bag."

"It's okay."

We walk together in the glassed corridor.

It seems as if we neither of us feel angry with Cori. We don't want to fall out with her. We like her. It's just the pain she causes that's the problem. Once her family is sorted out everything will be fine. Life will be just like it used to be when Cori and I first met. Then I won't be unhappy anymore because I'll get skinny and have friends!

Life will be perfect.

7

"Jasmine," Cori says.

She uses my name, my full name. There is something wrong.

"Could I have a word?"

"Yep, sure. Hang on," I say trying to be casual. I mess about with my bag to gain time as I have no idea what it is about but it's going to be bad.

We walk outside the form room and to the top of the stairs. Is she going to push me down them and then proclaim her innocence to everyone at my funeral?

She doesn't say anything for a minute. There is a teacher talking to two girls. She flashes her banana smile and her hair shimmers and waves to them as they walk past us.

"How dare you say things about my dad?" Her voice is even and her face calm. Despite the apparent anger her angel image is intact for those who care to take a look.

I feel like shouting to the people walking past, "Hey, look. This girl is amazing. All you see is what an angel she is but underneath she's full of hate." Instead I try to defend myself.

"I told Beth because she was concerned about

you and I had no idea it was a secret. You didn't tell me not to tell anyone," I say. "I wouldn't have told anyone if I'd known it was a secret but I honestly didn't know."

She stares with disbelief and disgust.

"You ever spread rumours around about me and I'll spread ones about you that will kill you."

I try to look as if I don't care.

We stand for a minute in the silence of the glass hollow. These are the glass windows that echo and throw the rumours at me. It's the echo glass.

She has always been an expert in giving dirty looks and this one is no exception. Then she says, "This is not the last of it. If you carry on like this you'll have no friends left, in fact I think that's already happened." And she walks down the stairs, leaving me at the hideous top, able to see a birds eye view of her head.

I walk on the tiles, stamping my feet as hard as possible. I feel so angry and confused.

Beth is in the form-room and I sit down next to her.

"She's just told me off for telling you about her dad when I didn't even know it was supposed to be a secret." I don't look at Beth, I stare at the two glass circles in the door before I notice her.

"I feel like crying!" she says in fierce words that I've never heard from her before.

She leaps off the table and runs to door. She flings it open so that it hits the side of the wall. Then it slowly falls back and sits in the doorframe. I can see her standing out there through the glass circles. She's with Cori who seems to have appeared from nowhere. They're smiling. Or are they laughing?

I don't know what to think, except that Beth and Cori seem to be best friends now and that I have no one. Everybody in the form is staring at me and they assume everything is my fault. It's always my fault.

"You always make people cry," says Ruth. I try to ignore them. I haven't done anything wrong.

I stay at my desk and stare through the two glass holes and watch Beth and Cori leave. I hope that the eyes of the class will soon be diverted. But it's too much to hope for.

Ruth's new best friend, Lucy, looks over at me with utter disgust. She reminds me of the looks I get on non-school uniform days. I can never get it right. I always have the wrong clothes. The wrong everything.

Ruth stands up, her yellow strands flowing around her, "Get out!" she screams.

I don't move. I can't.

"Let me help," she says, sharply grabbing my arm.

"But what has this got to do with you?" I ask.

"You disturb the peace and everyone hates you. Cori doesn't deserve what you do to her."

I stare at the class.

"Fine, we'll take a vote on it then shall we?" She lets go of my arm and marches to the front of the classroom by the blackboard. She stands tall and confident. "Put up your hand if you want Jasmine Harwood out of here." She looks out at the sea of faces amongst the red desks. "Keep them up so that Jasmine can see she has no friends."

She laughs. "Look Jas," she says. "Come and stand next to me."

I walk over to her and she links her arm through mine. "You see this? No one likes you, we don't like people who spread lies about our friends and then try to hurt them."

I look down at the floor because she has got it so wrong.

She yanks my black ponytail, "KEEP LOOKING!" she shouts. "WE HATE YOU. NOW GET OUT!"

No matter how much I want my legs to move they won't. She clutches the top of my arm and violently walks me to the door. How I hate the excess fat on my arms. She must be able to feel it. The door is flung open and she pushes me through it. I stand and watch through the glass circles. The whole class is laughing although I can't hear them.

I see my English teacher, Mrs Dorrian in the corridor. "Miss is there anything I can help with?"

"Actually, there is, Jasmine. If you could go to room five and put the pile of books in the stockroom I'd be ever so grateful." I smile. I can get away from the people who hate me and I can cry without them laughing at my tears.

It doesn't take long for rumours to be spread, and for Ione and her friends to get involved. At the end of the day, I go to collect my coat from my locker. It's hot, and the sun is streaming in through the windows even at three fifteen in the afternoon.

I click my padlock shut and put on my light coat. I am determined not to let Cori get to me this time. I've let her do too much harm to me already and I'm not going to let her do anything else to me.

I open the door with the glass circles in and

find myself at the top of the stairs. I walk down a few steps, turning with them. I notice a crowd of people standing at the foot.

Ione is there but Cori isn't. The other faces are familiar, but not enough to put names to.

"Why do you spread lies about my family?" Ione asks. She doesn't wait for an answer; obviously it isn't a question. "You do it for attention. You do everything for attention, that's why you went on that diet. You're so stupid." She turns her head away from my face.

I have nothing to say because they are not here to listen. They start to talk to each other as if I'm not here.

"If she were dead, no one would go to her funeral!" They all start to laugh.

I walk towards them so that I can push through and get home.

"Where do you think you're going?"

"Home," I say defiantly.

"We'll get you for this," someone screams.

I turn around, full of anger and say sharply, "I haven't done anything wrong. I told a concerned friend something I didn't know was a secret. Where's the crime in that?"

"Liar!"

I carry on walking. I have to get away.

I want to turn back and scream in their ears until they are deaf. Then I want to pull each of their heads off and throw them on the floor, stamping on them and pouring their brains and blood on the tiles. I wouldn't feel any of the pain they'd caused me if I did that.

I carry on walking out of school and all the way home. I lose my breath being so angry and walking so fast. But I will not stop. The world hates me.

I can't eat when I'm home. There are the Jaffa cakes I usually eat at four o'clock but I can't touch them. I pick up an apple and go to my room. There's no one here to know I'm not eating. Mum is staying late at the office tonight.

The dial on the scale reads six stone four pounds. I've met my goal and gone beyond. But the Alien is still here and my life is not perfect.

I bite into the apple and crunch. I'm not hungry and I can feel all the anger and upset filling my throat as if it were closing up. The Jaffa cakes sit downstairs, uneaten and I feel proud. I also feel guilty and confused. I do want to eat them really. The pain begins to shoot through me in intense waves. I throw the apple into the bin. I've only had one bite but I have to stop the pain.

I sit down to write my diary, to purge the thoughts and feelings:

Monday 21st June, Year 8.
Dear Diary,

I plod into school every day as regular as the tide. Cori and I are still not speaking. Hardly anybody is talking to me.

Maybe I should tell a teacher like Mum told me to do ages ago. Mrs Corcoran, (she's the head of Lower school) and she's quite nice but I just don't think anybody will take me seriously. All the teachers think Cori is great, she always gets high grades in her work. No one would believe she could be like this.

No, I've decided I'll stick it out rumour after rumour spreading from person to person. (You know they still haven't given up on the Nathan rumours!) There are others about me being anorexic too. I don't have any choice but to ignore them all.

When I got home from school I weighed six stone four pounds – Yay! But I still need to try hard at my diet. I'll cope much better if I do.

It's such a relief to have got down to six stone four pounds today because it has been so difficult to lose weight recently. I don't understand why. The dial on the scales just hasn't been going in the downwards direction very easily. At least I'm less now and I can smile and feel pleased. Of course, I still need to try harder: more exercise, less food which means I have to spread the butter thinly on my bread and to eat no chocolate at all. The weight should just drop off from now on!

Only a few more weeks until the end of term. I need to hold out until then. After that I have six weeks to do nothing in.

Love,
Jas xxx

The last day of term arrives. I walk around the corridor, keeping away from my form. They are determined to be bitchy right to the end.

I walk aimlessly around the glass corridors. The sun pours in, melting me. Once I've walked through the doors and am outside I see the sun standing with pride. Everything is golden and the grass is wilting with dryness. Without food plants die. Maybe the roots from the Alien inside me will also die. *So much for thanking me*, It says. And I remember the Alien does this to me to make me thin. I am thankful.

I saunter to the grass bank and walk to the foot. Nobody from school can see me here. I sit down facing the fence. Looking through it I can see the cars driving past. I wonder where all these cars are going to and what do these people think. Are they happier than me?

"Jasmine Harwood," comes a voice from behind.

I recognise it and feel weak and dizzy at the sound of it. There doesn't seem to be anywhere I can hide. My head turns towards the voice. I clamber to my feet.

The sun is shining brightly in my eyes preventing me from seeing properly. There are a crowd of girls, the same girls who were at the bottom of the stairs. Ione's voice keeps springing to life but I can't see which shadow is her's.

I stand paralysed.

Someone's hand comes out towards me and pushes me into the fence. I feel the wire threads stick through my uniform.

"No one makes trouble for my friends," the person says.

I am blind. I'm pushed against the wire that pokes ruthlessly into my back.

I can't feel the pain.

"You're a grass aren't you? You told Mrs Corcoran lies just to get attention."

"No," I say trying to proclaim my innocence. Suddenly I feel the roots inside me and hear It agreeing with all that they are saying.

Am I innocent?

"You've only heard one side of the story, what about mine?"

"Go on then."

I stand there, seeing their shadows. No words will come. When I open my mouth to try and speak, nothing is there. I look up at the school. The sun is in the way but I can see the glass building of the school shining colours I've never seen before. I wonder if I were to shout for help I would shatter the school to shards.

I don't call out.

I close my eyes for a minute then open them again and look at where the shine comes from.

Out of the blinding sun comes an angel, a halo above its head and its face serene. A smile I could mistake for satisfaction. I close my eyes and shut out the words that are being thrown at me.

Has God sent an angel to come and save me?

I tense all my muscles as if expecting someone to hit me. When my eyes open the shadows of the figures have moved away and the angel comes to me.

The figures stretch up the hill and leave me solo with the angel. It comes nearer to me, floating. Only stopping when it is almost touching.

A cloud must drift in the sky because a shadow forms over us. I can see the angel in more detail, the smile that can't be mistaken for anything but the upturned banana and the only imperfection of brown, bushy eyebrows meeting in the middle. I see the angel to be Corisande.

I gape at her shining face. It is frighteningly cold within its glow. I stare because I can't think of anything to say.

She stares back.

We stand in the surreal silence of the field as if we were mesmerised with studying a great statue. Her holy glow scares me because she hasn't been sent to save me. She looks at me because she despises me.

A shrill sound comes from the glass and I start to walk towards it, trying to ignore Cori.

"I hate you," are the words she keeps dropping from her mouth as she walks reluctantly by my side, towards school.

I don't say anything but keep looking at the frail glass so that I won't lose sight of my aim.

"Did you hear me or are you deaf as well as dumb?" Her words are violent but still her face is calm and glows. "I'm going to kill you," are the last words she can say to me before we enter the glass.

Part Two

Friends

8

Tick, tick. Drip, drip. The sounds alternate, fighting to sing solo. The rain falls against the window and the clock ticks, neither will cease and give the other that chance. I open my curtains and see the wind swaying the trees, bending them as if they're as athletic as cats.

The clock ticks to seven thirty. I sit on my bed and stare into the mirror attached to my dressing table. The pale face stares back at me as if I were a ghost haunting my bedroom. My dark hair clings limply to my face, concealing the hollows in my cheeks.

I pull off my pink night-dress and fold it neatly under the pillow. Picking up my school uniform from my desk chair I button the cream shirt and feel so pleased to find that the material gathers generously around my arms. I seem to have got thinner. My navy skirt, size twenty-two inches, is slightly too big!

I see the girl in the mirror smile slightly and the hollows in her cheeks move to become dimples, stretching the skin around her face as if there isn't quite enough to form a smile. The taut yellow skin conceals any feelings left inside. The two snakes which rest on her shoulders and lead to her neck are more prominent. She isn't a girl, she isn't Jasmine, she is a shape. A shape that is still too fat but that is making progress.

At eight o'clock the radio comes on and I go to have breakfast. I lift the milk out of the fridge and then put the box of cereal and a bowl out onto the table. I pour the milk and it slops around in the bottom of the china. The cereal falls against the sides of the bowl, clattering aimlessly to its early morning swim. The silver spoon dips and lifts and drops the cereal. One by one the flakes are lifted onto the spoon and are put into the bin. No food contaminates my body so early in the day.

I collect my books and put them in my bag and then I set out for my early morning walk to school. One foot then the next. I've started to count so that I can't think. I don't know what I'm counting but the rhythm is comforting. I need to hear the numbers in my head.

At the bottom of Garret Bell I stare up at the glass shape that echoes rumours and glistens with colours. The school is a shape that illuminates the sky and looks inviting. But it is also the echo glass where rumours and pain never die.

The November weather is cold and I pull my coat closely to me before setting off up the hill. The rain steadily falls against me.

"Jasmine, wait for me."

I turn around and see the breathless china doll running towards me.

"Beth, how are you?"

"I'm okay. What about you?"

"I'm fine." I stare at her bulging eyes and she turns them away from me.

In her porcelain words she says, "Promise you

won't laugh."

"Of course."

"There's this really nice lad on my estate who I like." She doesn't look at me but seems to find the ground greatly interesting.

"Why would I laugh at that?"

"I don't know."

"I still like Nathan. How sad is that?" We laugh and walk together.

We are in a different form room from last year. It is smaller and darker. We have a tall, thin window at one end of the room but it lets little light in, especially as the sun sits low in the sky at this time of the year. The tables are brown and the sky outside is dark.

Cori comes to the form. "Hello," she says in her gushy voice.

I still envy her soft words and her ability to say the right things.

She puts her arms around me and I put mine around her. This is our morning hug. We pull away and I look past her glow and know we will never be best friends again.

"Have you lost weight?" Her words feel more like an accusation than a question. How I wish I could make the alien feeling root inside her for a while. Not for long but just so that she could feel this pain. I hear myself sigh quietly. I'm past wanting revenge, I'm trying to be mature now.

"No," I bite back.

"Yes you have, you're all bone." She looks at me in disgust, looking me up and down just as they had on the non-school uniform days. It feels as if she knows there's an Alien inside me and is searching for it.

I hold back the harsh words which are filling

my mind. I move slightly away from her. I need my space. When I turn to see if Beth is still there Cori does her disappearing act.

"Probably gone to find Ione," I say to Beth. I hope she moves into her form."

"Me too."

I am prepared to be friends with Cori on the surface but that's as far as it goes. I spend all my time with Beth now and she doesn't want to hang around with Cori either. But Cori's still popular with the rest of the form even though she hangs around with Ione and her friends all the time.

Mrs Corcoran stands threateningly over us in Year 9 assembly. She says, "Nurse Ratcliffe is the designated nurse for this school. You may recognise her from when you had the Rubella injection."

We all remember having that injection.

"She'll be coming in every Thursday to see everyone in Year 9. She'll be discussing any concerns with you that you may have. She's here to promote healthy life-styles which includes eating, exercise and no smoking."

She'll see everyone?

I'm scared.

Each Thursday I dread. After every week I relax until the next one comes along and I wonder if it'll be me. I want her to tell me I have a problem and that she can help me but being found out is a terrifying thought.

I think she'll have been told about me. The teachers suspect there are problems because they treat me as if I will break with one wrong word. To what extent they know about things, I can only guess.

"I want you to read chapter five for next lesson," says Mrs Dorrian at the end of the lesson. Her red hair is let loose in waves of energy. Beth and I like English. We're glad to have her for the third year running. She seems to have hair to match her enthusiasm.

I pick up my book and my folder to put them in my bag. "Oh no," I say.

"What?" Beth says.

"I was so good this morning."

"What are you going on about?"

"I've left my lunch at home." I sigh deeply, perhaps over dramatically.

"So why does that make you good?"

"I made my own lunch. I was feeling pleased with myself. If I let Mum make my sandwiches she doesn't use the low fat spread."

"You're so silly."

"No just cautious. Oh well."

"Mrs Dorrian?"

"Yes, Bethany?"

I look at Beth with something I hope will either kill her or stop her from saying what I think she's going to say.

"Miss, Jasmine's left her lunch at home by mistake. She doesn't know what to do."

"Oh dear, Jasmine," she says turning to me, her red hair flying towards me. "I can lend you some money. I know it can be a pain to wait in the long queue to get a ticket from the dinner lady. I've left my lunch at home before now!" She laughs. "Come and find me at lunch time and I'll come with you to the canteen."

I wait until she's gone into the stockroom before I speak.

"Thanks, Beth," I say sarcastically.

"Well, we can't have you starving all day can we?"

I give Beth a look of exasperation.

I have an hour before lunch and there's no getting out of it, Beth's going to make sure of that.

We walk down the corridor in an uncomfortable three. People are beginning to dribble into the canteen when we get there.

I choose an egg roll.

"I'll pay you back tomorrow, Miss," I say.

"No problem," she calls out as people begin to push between us.

I like her but I'm glad to get away.

The room is full of blue tables cluttered with dinner plates and drinks scattered over them. Beth and I find a table to sit at. We don't say anything until I notice Mrs Dorrian has sat not far away.

"I don't believe this," I say.

"What now?"

"Mrs Dorrian's sitting over there."

"Where?"

"I can't exactly point at her can I?" I pause to see if she can see her. "By the window," I say.

I watch her point her bulging eyes in the direction of the window. I stare intently at her face and then we both giggle.

"I think she might be watching you," Beth finally says and I know this is a chance I can't miss.

I pick up my roll and eliminate hunger. I eat all of it. I hate myself for it. There will be no more leaving my lunch at home after this, I'll always double check.

Once I'm home I look at the entry I'd written in my diary a few days ago about throwing my lunch away. A diary really is a useful reference book!

Wednesday 16th November, Year 9.
Dear Diary,
I'm really very good at throwing my lunch away without anyone knowing and I do lose some weight! I'm beginning to see that the Alien was right all along, the more weight I lose the more It leaves me alone. Although the horrible feelings haven't completely gone yet.
The bubble of hunger sits in my stomach and I wait for it either to explode or implode. I hate the noise it makes but hunger makes me feel as if I am succeeding in something. I am permitted to smile.
Love,
Jas xxx

The rain seems to be almost permanent through November. It drips onto the ground during the day and the night. The sky seems to grow darker and duller causing the form room to look uninviting.

When the glass school is subjected to this gloominess the days seem endless.

My diary entries don't seem to have helped unravel the knotted ball of wool like I'd hoped they would when I first started to write. Is there any point in adding to the confusion by writing even more in the book? I suppose one day it might all make sense.

9

The dull December sun shines in the sky between the clouds which are pushed by the wind.

One cold January morning a letter comes for me through morning registration. A brown envelope sits in the middle of the attendance sheets and blue biro scrawls 'Jasmine Harwood.' I wait for the teacher to come to take the register and give me the envelope.

It's handed to me and I say, "Thank you." I know what it is because it's Thursday morning. I open it and a printed slip stares back at me. I'm supposed to go to the medical room at eleven thirty. I put it back in the brown envelope.

I'm nervous and I don't want to see the nurse but I also look forward to seeing her with a strange hope.

My appointment means I will miss some of my IT lesson. I calculate that it will take twenty minutes as I discover that's how long everybody else has been in there for.

I walk to the medical room, counting my steps as I go down the corridors and up the stairs. I take my seat outside and wait until the person in there has come out. The chair is black and would have stuck to my legs if I weren't wearing tights. It creaks when I move but I can't sit still because I'm nervous.

The January weather makes the school

almost as cold as the Arctic or what I imagine it'd be like being shut inside a freezer. I sit shivering from coldness and shaking from nerves. It doesn't look good.

"Jasmine Harwood?" a woman asks.

I look up. "Yes."

"Do you want to come in?"

I want to say no but I follow her anyway. She's very tall and has dull blonde hair falling down her back. She wears pink lipstick and her eyes seem to shine. It seems wrong to feel hopeful.

"Take a seat." She points to the chair by the side of her desk. She sits at the desk where there are files piled up. There is a pen so she will clearly be writing notes while I'm there.

"I'm seeing everyone in Year 9 just to discuss any concerns they may have or anything they want to talk about. I'm also going to be here every Thursday lunchtime for an Open Clinic. It's so that anybody can come and see me if they're worried or need to talk to someone. It can be about boyfriends or teacher trouble. I'm just here for people and to help if I can."

I nod to show that I'm understanding.

"Right," she says in a final sort of way. Her voice is brisk, but not formal. "Can you take off your shoes for me and we'll measure your height first."

I bend over and unbuckle my shiny black dolly shoes. I slip each shoe off and put them neatly, lining them up, under the table. I lift my head and stand. I feel stupid because she's watched me precisely lining up my shoes.

I stand against the door. Something sits above my head because she pulls it down and reads off a measure. "Are you standing straight?"

"Yep."

"Five feet four inches and a half."

I suddenly feel much happier because I'm taller than when I was last measured at the doctors. I have grown another inch.

Being an inch taller means I'm not as fat at this weight as I was when I was five foot three inches.

I stand away from the door and she jots it down in my file. "Would you pop onto the scales for me?"

I was six stone ten pounds this morning. Yet more weight that I've gained recently. I'm not sure what she will make of that. I put my feet on the scales and stare down at the dial.

The dial spins so fast. I wonder when it will stop. The numbers keep getting higher and higher. A sick feeling grows inside me.

"Forty-four kilograms."

I try to work it out but I can't. "How much is that in stones?"

"It's about seven stones."

I'm more on her scales than I am at home.

We sit down again and she draws a chart. "You see this?" she says pointing at the blue paper which the chart sits on.

I nod.

"It's telling me you're underweight."

I am pleased.

"It isn't anything to worry about."

I am not pleased.

"It means we'll just have to try and raise your weight slightly. You're about a stone underweight at the moment." She puts the paper back into the file. "I'd like you to keep a food diary for me.

That way we can see what you're eating and whether it's enough. We also need to find out if you're eating the right sort of foods. When you've filled it out I'll give it to the dietician who'll look at it properly."

I stare at my hands. I'm no good at giving eye contact.

"I need to know everything you eat; food and drink. It's no good eating differently to how you normally would. Try to keep it as normal as possible."

I nod again.

"Is there anything you would like to talk about?"

"I don't think so," I mumble.

"Ok," she says. "Come and see me again next Thursday with your food diary and we'll talk about that."

"Ok."

I get up and open the door. Has she caught me? Does she know?

I look at my watch, I've been in there for an hour. She hasn't even asked me any of the questions that she's apparently asked all the others: food, drugs and smoking.

Keeping a food diary is not easy. Food written down on paper makes me realise I am eating extraordinarily large quantities. I keep the sheets of paper with me all the time: at the dinner table and at school so that I don't forget things.

"What are those sheets?" asks Mum.

"My food diary."

"I think it's silly she's told you to keep that thing."

She picks up her plate and takes it to the

sink. "Hurry up and eat your dinner."

"I have to keep them, the nurse told me to." I push the potato under its skin and eat the salad. I place my knife and fork together with a satisfying clash on the sides of the plate.

I get up and leave the kitchen before she finds the food hidden under my potato skins.

I fill out my food diary for the whole week. By the end of it I can see where I need to cut down. I am eating too much chocolate.

I look at the hardback diary. How many more pages do I have to fill before it's finished? It looks like loads! I flick through the pages with words on and stop at an entry I'd written three months ago.

Saturday 5th October, Year 9.
Dear Diary,

Since I've been dieting I hardly ever go out. But the strange thing is, I don't care! I still keep my camera with me all the time because I still want to be a photographer, but a skinny one. Maybe one day I could be a famous photographer and have exhibitions in the Art Gallery.

I wonder if I'll be like this next year, or if I'll have reached thinness and be happy.

Imagine that.

I feel so depressed all the time at the moment. I even cry when I don't know why I'm crying. I guess that means the Alien is making sure that I lose more weight to be happy.

Love,
Jas xxx

***

"How are you, Jasmine?" asks Nurse Ratcliffe. Thursday has arrived.

"Fine," I mumble.

I sit down on the plastic chair and pull my food diary out of my bag.

"Here it is," I say, handing her the white sheets of A4.

"Oh, thank you. Did you eat in a relatively normal way?"

I nod.

She looks at each day, her white hands turning each page. I see my blue fountain pen ink. I hate it because I have written it and, more to the point, I had *eaten* it.

"At a glance I'd say you're not eating quite enough." She pauses for a minute. "You are perhaps eating too much fat."

FAT. Too much fat.

My mind is working overtime and the word fat keeps flashing inside. The pain gets nauseatingly worse. The intensity of these feelings seem to be killing me.

I have to stop eating fat. The fat is what makes me weigh so much.

She is watching me. "You've written here that you had half a sandwich at break time. How about a whole sandwich?"

"It's a bit too much."

"Okay. What about bananas? They're a healthy choice. Could you eat that instead of chocolate?"

"I don't like bananas."

"Okay. Well we need to think about alternatives. I'll give this to the dietician and then we'll have a better idea about where we can improve your diet."

She looks at me and smiles. "Well, we'll leave it here for now."

I stand up.

"You don't mind putting on weight for me do you?"

I open the door slightly. "No," I say and I walk out of the room.

10

A small girl sits quietly in the corner of the Science Lab. I look at her. "Beth?"

"Yeah?"

"What's that girl's name?"

"I can't remember what the teacher said it was."

"I feel sorry for her. I'm going to talk to her."

I stand up and begin to walk over to her, my science overall flapping around my uniform. I walk past the ferocious sounds of the Bunsen burners giving out their heat to the experiments sitting on the tripods. Some of the containers have bubbles flowing over the top of them.

"Hello," I say nervously.

She looks up at me and smiles weakly. Her black hair had concealed her face from me. Now that I stand towering over her I can see that her face is small and her eyes are too. She looks a bit scared.

"My name's Jasmine," I say. "My friends call me Jas. You can call me Jas if you like." I feel stupid. "What's your name?"

"Adelaide," she says in a tiny voice that barely reaches my ears.

"Ade, what?"

"Adelaide Millis. Call me Ade, if you like."

"OK. What school are you from?"

"Oh just a school in Cardiff where I used to live."

"Oh wow! I've never been there."

"We move around a lot cuz of my Dad's work. But this is the last move now so that I can get my GCSEs."

"My friend's over there. You see the one with blonde hair?" I point at her. "Her name's Bethany. Why don't you come and sit with us. We can't leave you here on your own, you look so lonely."

"All right." She looks more at ease and less quiet. I feel good that I have made a new friend.

She follows me past the tables where the Bunsen burners flare. The girl with angel tendencies stands watching, torn between her experiment and watching me with Adelaide. She looks at home amongst the fire.

We sit down at the bench and draw a table to record our results in. Beth stirs the experiment on the tripod.

"Since you're new to the school, you need to know about its history."

She looks interested and nods eagerly.

"Well," I say, taking a deep breath, "Rumour has it that before the school was built there was a huge house sitting here. And the coal house was the safest place to be in the war."

I watch her olive coloured hands push the ruler neatly onto the correct part of the page and then draw a perfectly straight line.

"The Garret family who lived there were killed in the war. So there was just this old woman who was a recluse. And so when she died nobody knew about it for weeks. It wasn't until the milkman and postman went to the house and noticed a terrible smell that they smelt something fishy."

Beth beams over the frothing experiment, "That's a good one, Jas!"

"Thank you," I say as I stand up to give a curtsey.

Adelaide smiles too.

"Before you carry on with the story, record the temperature of one-hundred degrees as the starting point. I'm now taking it off so that we can record the cooling temperatures."

Ade writes the temperature down.

"Anyway," I say carrying on with the story. "When they went inside the house they found it was empty except for a small table in the dingy attic. On this shabby table was a glass bell but when one of the men picked it up to ring it, it made no sound. Apparently there wasn't a clapper inside."

"So what about the old woman's body?" Ade asks.

"The body was found there too, next to the table where the bell was. They say that the house went up for sale but no one would buy it because they thought it was haunted. The price kept coming down until the local authority took it and built the school. Someone suggested calling it Garret Bell to keep the ghosts of the family away. They said that the school had to remember the past so that the ghosts would be at peace. And that's all I know."

"Ooh eerie," Ade says and I smile.

"Yeah right, Jas! You have such a way with

words to exaggerate everything like that." She laughs.

"It's not exaggerated," I say. "That's the real reason why the school is called Garret Bell."

"Yeah it is. But there weren't any dead bodies."

"Well, that's what everyone told me."

"Sucker!"

I pull my tongue out at her as she looks at the thermometer again.

Then Beth looks at Ade, "Some of it's true. But when you're as good at English as Jas is she'll make everything else up."

"You calling her a liar?" Ade asks. She seems more interested now. Now that there seems to be untruth in my words.

"Oh no. They're not lies. Just an exaggerated story. Anyway, it sounded really good," she says nudging me.

I have to see the nurse every Thursday. She doesn't seem worried about me. She only weighs me when she can be bothered. She's often away doing injections in other schools so there are a lot of long gaps before I have to see her again.

"Pop onto the scales for me," she says.

It seems today is one of those rare moments that she wants to weigh me.

The Alien hits me by making my heart beat fast. It hurts. I try to remember what I weighed this morning. Six stone eight pounds. That would make me six stone ten pounds on her scales. Why can't all scales be the same?

The Alien hates me for standing on those brown scales. I know It doesn't like it because it hurts each time I cooperate.

"You've lost weight," she says this morning.

I watch her plot the graph on the blue paper. I don't say anything.

"Have you eaten your break yet?"

"No."

"Hmm, maybe that's why you weigh less today."

"Probably," I say wondering why she's helping me to lie.

I leave the nurse feeling proud that she hasn't found me out but I'm also annoyed that she sees nothing wrong.

I sit with Ade in the form when I get back. We're all making our No Smoking posters.

"I'll go and find Beth because she can draw some cool things," I say. I don't like sitting down for long and this is a good excuse. Standing up as much as possible means I get to burn off more calories.

"Will you glue this before you get her?" she asks.

I pick up the glue and pull at the top. The top won't come off and I don't have the strength to pull. "Sorry, Ade, you'll have to get the top off."

The strength in my fingers has gone. And even breathing seems to take too much effort. It means I am succeeding with cutting down on the food. That is no bad thing.

I pass the glue back to her. She takes it and pulls the top off without any trouble.

She doesn't look at me and I am too ashamed to say anything so I stick the picture she's cut out onto the cardboard in front of her. I rub the uneven glue behind the paper so that it will be smooth.

"I'll go and get Beth now, shall I?"

She nods her head but doesn't stop colouring in the next drawing of a packet of cigarettes.

I stand up but feel my head spin. I hold onto the back of my chair to regain some balance before venturing across the classroom. I'd feel so ashamed if I collapsed in front of the whole class. Imagine that.

Mum tells me that Nurse Ratcliffe phoned her today.

"I wasn't in the office when she phoned so I have to ring back to arrange a time with her," she says.

I don't say anything.

"It'll have to be in the evening. I'm just not available any other time." Pause. "I'll tell her exactly what I think about you doing those food diary things. It just makes you more self conscious about what you're eating. You're only fourteen you shouldn't be thinking about what you're eating."

"She said that I eat too much fat."

"Rubbish! Rubbish! I want this nonsense to stop. I've had enough of it."

She opens the cupboard door and selects a pudding. A Marks & Spencer Chocolate sponge cake with gooey icing.

It is filled with calories. It is filled with fat.

I can't live here with food like that trying to tempt me.

Thursday 22nd February, Year 9.
Dear Diary,
My mum is trying to make me fat. You should have seen the chocolate cake she made me eat for tea. I can feel it inside me, bubbling away in my

stomach just being consumed and sent to all my fat cells to be made even fatter.

It's unbearable.

I felt really faint at school today. It must have been the evil looks that Cori keeps giving me. I don't think she likes me being friends with Ade and Beth. Actually I don't think she wants me to have any friends at all.

Must lose weight.

Love,

Jas xxx

11

Beth and Ade find me in the form room at lunchtime.

"Jas, the nurse wants to see you."

"What for?"

"A hearing test."

I look at them. I don't believe their words.

"As if," I say as I walk towards my table.

I look up to see if they're still there but they've disappeared.

I'm alone in the classroom. I reach into my school bag and retrieve my diary. I take it with me everywhere because I expect to be alone so much of the time. Even though I do have friends I always feel alone because they can't understand me. My diary is my only trustworthy friend.

Friday 12th March, Year 9.
Dear Diary,

I'm alone again. Ade and Beth have told me that the nurse wants to see me for a hearing test. I feel so scared.

I told them I didn't believe them. I don't believe them. But what if the nurse is in the medical room right now waiting for me?

I feel so sick just thinking about it.

When my friends do this to me I realise that I don't need anyone but you.

Oh, got to go they've come back...

I close the diary and try to push all my thoughts away.

I stand up and they wait for me to walk to them.

"We're going for a walk," Ade says, "You wanna come?"

I nod.

"Do you like my nails?" Beth asks as we walk along the corridors surrounded with the glass walls.

"Wow, they look so cool," I say looking at her blue nails.

"If you grew your nails a bit they might look even nicer," Ade says.

"I know," Beth says, holding her nails up to her eyes. "My mum would kill me if she knew I was wearing this. It'd be even worse if they were any longer than this."

"I know what you mean, I'm not allowed to wear it either. But how can you hide blue?" I say with a giggle.

We open the door leading outside to the back of the school and we walk straight to the small wall by the music rooms.

"You should have said before," Ade says. "I could have brought some nail-varnish remover in. Hey, we could do this everyday. We'd paint our nails in the morning and at home time we'd go the cloakrooms and take it off!"

I hear someone playing the piano in the distance and in another room there is someone else trying to learn the guitar. The two sounds merge with each other and make no musical sense.

"What about the teachers?"

"What about them?"

We all laugh. They look comfortable laughing but I feel uneasy.

"Can I change the subject for a sec," I say, staring at the trees swinging in the wind.

They look at me full of attention. I see Adelaide put her hand on her skirt to stop it from flying up in the wind. I almost smile but under these circumstances it wouldn't be right.

"The nurse wants to speak to my mum."

"Really?" Beth says, "How come?"

"I've no idea."

"Do you think it's going to be bad?" Ade asks.

"I just don't know." I feel the pain surging up into my throat forming an uncomfortable lump. "I'm worried," I say almost as a whisper that is lost in the wind.

"So would I be," Beth says.

We stay sitting on the cold wall.

"Perhaps it's just the hearing test," Beth says, trying to be optimistic.

"Or maybe she's got some books for you," Ade says.

"Well, it could be but why would she go through my mum and not straight to me?"

"I guess you'll find out soon," Ade says.

The clock ticks to seven o'clock. The dreaded time that the nurse is coming to speak to Mum.

I hear the car door slam and the nurse walking down the path. Mum opens the door and then I hear them walking together away from the house.

I go to the spare bedroom to look out of the window. It's too dark to see anything.

I listen to the rain against the window as I sit on the bed. The mirror faces me and I stare into it trying desperately to stay calm.

Twenty minutes have ticked past and then I hear the front door close. I stand up and breathe deeply. I push my waist-length hair behind my shoulders and pray my voice will be strong and not weak with nerves. I walk down each step.

"Am I allowed to know what the nurse wanted?" I ask tentatively.

"Of course." She smiles. "She told me she was a bit worried because two girls approached her and told her that they'd seen you throwing your lunch away." She stops. "I presume they saw you throwing your crusts away."

"They must have," I say, wondering why she is helping me to hide the truth.

"Apparently they also said you didn't have enough strength to get the top off some glue."

I laugh. "That's because the top was glued down!" I hope to sound as if I really do find it funny.

"She'd like to see you next week"

"Oh, ok."

That's it. I don't have to be creative with excuses. The truth can stay hidden.

But now I know that Ade and Beth are to blame for talking to the nurse behind my back.

Friday 12th March– continued six and a half hours later:

I HATE THEM. THE BULLIES TOLD ON ME. I'd only told you earlier today I had no friends. It was

sooo true. I've had it with friends. They do nothing but hurt you!
ENOUGH!
Jas.

I walk sluggishly towards the fragile glass. The place where voices are spread ever onwards and always hurtful.

I want to cry, but I can't let my mascara run this early in the morning.

I walk into the dingy classroom and Ade and Beth both come running up to me.

"What happened with the nurse then?" They hold onto my arms and almost say it synchronised as if they've been practising.

"I thought you were going to phone to tell me," Beth says, her eyes looking full of hurt.

"Sorry," I say, "Mum was around and I didn't want her listening."

I pause. I need breath. I need space.

"The nurse tried to tell my mum that I wasn't eating properly," I say. "She said that some girls approached her. Do you know who they could be?"

"I've no idea, Jas," Ade says. "Sorry. But it means people are noticing you and your weird ways, so be careful."

I'd hoped they'd own up.

As always, lunchtime arrives too soon. I put my hand inside my bag, feel around for my sandwiches and tuck them up the sleeve of my navy, baggy cardigan. The bin is conveniently positioned by the door. I walk purposefully to the door, pretending I'm going somewhere important. As I reach the door, my arm flies above the bin and the sandwiches fall out of the sleeve of my cardigan and into the bin. The flying sandwiches sometimes remind me of Cori throwing Beth's bag out of the window last summer.

No one ever notices. I am a pro.

At quarter past one Ade says, "I've just got to take the bin down."

"I didn't know you're on bin duty today," I say feeling confused.

"Yeah. Unfortunately. Tis so shameful the way everyone stares at me when I've got my hand out in front of me while holding my nose with my other!" She laughs.

"I'll come with you." I want to distract her in case she sees my sandwiches.

"Sure."

We walk to the huge dustbins outside. She lifts the lid and the disgusting bin-smell immediately springs out and hits us.

Ade picks up the red plastic bin and begins to shake it around in front of her.

"What are you doing?" I want her to stop. If she carries on she'll find the sandwiches that can so easily be identified as mine. I feel my heart beating rapidly and my face getting hot with fear. The emptiness in my stomach spreads through every bone and I feel useless.

"Looking for your sandwiches."

"They're not in there. I ate them."

"We'll see," she says. She lifts the bin to the big dustbin. Then she tilts it very slightly so that the contents dribbles out and gives her the chance of seeing if my lunch is lying in there.

"Don't do that." She doesn't listen.

I put my hand out and hit the bin. She drops it and it falls to the floor with the contents spilling onto the ground.

My sandwiches sit innocently amongst other items and I hate them for being mine.

"You told me you'd eaten them!" she screams. Her face is full of anger and her eyes are wide.

"They're not mine," I say as I bend down and start to pick up the rubbish; apple cores, half eaten sandwiches and empty crisp packets.

"You're only doing this because you want people to tell you how gorgeous your body is."

"That's not true," I say, nearly crying.

I watch her walk up the steps and back into school. She turns around, "I'm going to a teacher now. This has gone too far."

Please tell someone, I think. Please let someone make this stop.

The Alien quickly steps in and It screams, *Stop her from telling someone. If you don't I'll make life hell for you. You think things are bad now but I can do worse!*

I hate It. But I know It makes sense.

I grab the bin and run up the steps, "Please don't," I call out. "Please, I promise you those sandwiches aren't mine. Ask anybody and they'll tell you I ate mine."

She looks at me with such pity. "Just this once," she says. "But if I ever find any food that's yours in that bin or find out that those sandwiches were yours then I'm going straight to a teacher."

I treasure the last chance she has given me.

My dream of falling down the stairs has diminished and has since been replaced by the overwhelming thoughts of becoming thinner. I imagine that I collapse at school. Everybody would know what was wrong and I wouldn't have to tell them.

The dream sometimes makes me die and other times I don't. The security that other people can offer makes it a dream of hope. If it really happened then I'd die knowing somebody cared.

I wonder if dreaming in this way makes me the person I was accused of being - only doing this for attention. I don't want attention. I want to be ignored but at the same time I want somebody to acknowledge this Alien inside.

Mum keeps moaning at me for not scraping my plate clean. It seems that they're all obsessed with food.

"Do you want to be anorexic?" she says nastily.

"No."

"Well I suppose you don't look half-starved."

I hate her for saying these words. Now there is no choice but to exercise all evening to make my legs thinner. My legs cause me much concern by the way that they wobble when I walk upstairs.

Sunday 21st March, Year 9.
Dear Diary,

I hate school. Cori's intent on telling everybody that I'm only dieting for attention. She tells everyone that they should ignore me, and Ione agrees with her. I wish they would ignore me.

They smile at me when I'm there but give me looks which feed the Alien when they think I'm not looking. They giggle in groups when they pretend they haven't seen me and talk loudly so that I can hear.

Cori told me months ago that she would kill me.

I'm still alive. I'm still waiting.

Jas xxx

12

Saturday 3rd April, Year 9.
Dear Diary,
    April is already here. The weather is still wet and the clouds look dull. The Easter holiday will be here soon.

    I'm so glad it's the weekend. School is so much more difficult at the moment. The form are always shouting accusations at me. They believe everything that Cori and Ione say about me.

    I want somebody to realise that something is wrong and to somehow make things better. But nobody notices how miserable I feel. The Alien constantly tells me that It is here to make me feel better. But I haven't got back down to six stones eight pounds. In fact, I just seem to keep on gaining even though I'm DEFINITELY not eating more. It's so depressing.

    I walk around the glassed corridors at break and lunchtimes. I have no real friends anymore since I can't trust Beth or Ade. I notice that the windows could so easily be broken and the cold floor can so easily kill. These hard surfaces seem to offer a strange hope.

    Love,
    Jas xxx

I still dream.

I dream that the glass will break in the corridors when I clench my hand into a fist and push it through the window.

It shatters to segments and falls with satisfying clashes across the ground outside.

Cori and Ione sometimes come into the dream and they laugh at me. Then they push me through the glass and I fall from the third floor to the ground. The glass smashes around me and falls as if it were the clapper that had been broken, falling through the hollow of the glass shell.

I'm lying on my back. Blood is the only colour left from the sun on the day it had blinded me on the field.

One more look at where I've fallen from and I see Cori and Ione peering down at me. Still smiling. Cori's angel is still intact even though I can see the evil inside her. Then I close my eyes and die.

It's lunch and I sit there dreaming about glass. Ade comes into the room, her eyes small, almost hidden inside her face as if it were a rose that's turning into a bud, hiding all the internal features.

"Mrs Corcoran wants to speak to you." Her voice is loud and clear.

"Why? What have I done?"

"I've told her about you not eating."

"WHAT!" I shout with what I hope will break through her.

"Come on. She said we can find a hole in her office to hide away in and just talk."

She grabs my arm and pulls me down the corridor. "What if I don't go, will she tell my mum?"

"Yes. I would come if I were you."

I follow her down the corridor.

My head is in a dull spin of thoughts. What will I say? Will I deny it? I just have to remember that I don't have a problem and I'm not on my own because the Alien is with me. But I'll admit to anything so long as she doesn't call Mum.

Ade knocks on the door and we wait until she opens it.

"Ah, come on in girls," she says kindly. I see a glimmer in her eyes.

Chairs are arranged in a circle. I pick the chair furthest away from them and sit on the edge for reassurance of a quick exit to the door if needed. I remember all the other times I've nearly been caught but I've always got out of them. There is a way out of this too. There is no doubt about it.

"Start from somewhere," she says kindly.

"I don't know what to say," I say staring at the coffee table.

"Adelaide tells me you've been throwing food away."

I don't say anything.

"She's worried about you." I look at Ade and hate her for doing this to me.

"You won't fall out with Adelaide for telling me, will you?"

I shake my head. I have no friends.

She leans over to me. Her voice has changed to a softer tone. She doesn't seem like the same person. It's as if the teacher who towers over our heads in assembly, screaming at the girls who refuse to be quiet, has died and this nice teacher has been resurrected.

She stretches out her hand and touches my wrist. I look up at Ade who's watching. I see her turn her head away.

"Goodness, you really are nervous. I can feel your pulse racing!" Mrs Corcoran says. "You must try and calm down."

I smile.

"Your mum needs to know."

I stop smiling. There has to be a way out of this.

"No she doesn't," I say.

She sighs and softly says, "How would you feel if Ade had stopped eating?"

But I haven't stopped eating. I'm not thin. I need to lose weight. Why would I lie to myself?

"What do you weigh?" she asks, changing the subject.

"Seven stones." I've gained weight. Again.

She stops talking but still holds onto my wrist as if she's making sure my heart won't stop beating.

Wasn't this what I wanted? Somebody at last is taking me seriously and trying to help but the bubble of nerves in my stomach has exploded and is spreading though my body. I'm not hungry anymore. I can't eat because the nerves have eaten away hunger.

I definitely don't want her help. It is all going wrong. Mum can't get involved because I know I'll be in so much trouble.

I try desperately hard to think about what to do.

The door suddenly springs open as if a strong

wind has pounded it. A mound of red floods into the room.

"Oh, I'm ever so sorry," Mrs Dorrian says when she sees the three of us sitting together.

"No, no it's ok. Come in," Mrs Corcoran says. She turns to me. "I have to tell Mrs Dorrian what's going on," she says half making an apology.

Mrs Dorrian sits down on the only vacant chair. There are no more light green coloured chairs in the room. We are all there, all because of me and I want to cry. I don't want any of this.

"Adelaide came to me because she's worried about Jasmine not eating."

She nods and then says, "But we already guessed you had an eating disorder."

I'm not sure how they guessed but I don't want to question it.

"We'll have to tell Nurse Ratcliffe. She already knows because Adelaide and Bethany have both told her." She pauses and then adds, "But you managed to find your way out of admitting to that one!" She almost laughs. Maybe she would have if it weren't on what they consider to be a serious subject.

"You have a choice, Jasmine," Mrs Corcoran says. "I can tell your mum for you or you can tell her. Either way she will have to come into school so that we can talk to her."

I consider my options for a moment and decide that she'll probably take it better from me. Besides there isn't much to tell. Not really.

"I'll tell her," I say.

"Ok. Well I've really got to go now but come and see me tomorrow to tell me what happens." She touches my arm again.

I look over at Mrs Dorrian who smiles eagerly from inside the red that frames her face.

I stand up. I'm going to find a way out of this and then I'll be laughing about it in a few months time.

I press the keys on the piano at home and listen to the noise each note makes while I wait for Mum to come back from work. Her car drives up outside and I go into the living room so that I can't see her.

The front door opens. "Hello!" she shouts and I appear in the hallway. She walks into the kitchen and puts her bags down.

I watch.

"Mrs Corcoran wants to speak to you."

"Why?"

"Well, you remember what happened with the nurse?"

She nods and says, "Yes, you've got to see her soon haven't you?"

I ignore the question and carry on with my original trail of thought. "Well the girls who went to see her have gone to speak to Mrs Corcoran and so she wants to speak to you now as well."

"I don't understand."

"They've told her I'm on a diet and she's a bit worried. I only told them I didn't mind losing a bit of weight."

"What do you mean you don't mind losing a bit of weight?" she shouts. She turns to face me and I watch her eyebrows meet in the middle the way Cori's do.

I feel trapped and I step backwards until I feel the wall pressing against my back.

"Do you want to be anorexic?" she says

harshly.

"No. Just speak to her," I say. I've given up trying to explain. I walk away. I can't say any more.

The last day of term arrives and Mrs Corcoran hasn't phoned. She asks if I've told her.

"Some of it," I say.

"Well, tell her properly in the holiday."

"Please don't make me. She got angry."

"She loves you, that's why. It'll be OK," and she pushes my hair behind my shoulder.

13

The holiday arrives and the rain continuously falls. I can't sleep because I'm worried about telling Mum. I have no dream to save me from reality.

I don't speak to Beth or Ade. I don't want to. I don't feel like doing anything.

I pull my wardrobe door open and see a blue, stretchy dress hiding in the corner. It feels comfortable because I know that I can eat without feeling how tight my clothes are on my waist.

I'm eating a lot now and I can't stop. I look down at my distending stomach and realise I have to keep the dress on. The sight of my flesh is far too frightening.

When the darkness swallows up the light I'm still wearing it. In the morning I wake up and see my stomach still protruding and covered in the blue fabric. I keep it on.

I cry and sit in bed, wondering what else to do to escape. I have a book that I try to read but I can't concentrate. I try to sleep but that's impossible. I have no dreams and nothing to create them with. There are no distractions. I stay in the warmth of my feather quilt that offers me safety for a short while.

Gradually I feel as if I can barely move. I lie here. Lifeless.

Tuesday 13ᵗʰ April, Year 9.
Dear Dairy,
I'm still in bed.
Time is running out, and the days are ticking by. Just like I'd been warned. I've tried to make the most of school and to enjoy it but it's still going too fast. I remember Mum's friends always used to say that school is the best years of your life. Does that mean life will always be this bad? Maybe if I try harder at my work I'll like school ... Oh what the hell do I do? I either have to find an escape or tell.
An escape. The only true escape is death.
Love,
Jas xxx

I run a bath. I peel off the dress for the first time in four days and allow the warm water to splash over my body. I hope it will purify it but the salt water from my eyes mixes with the bubbles. There are lots of white bubbles to hide my stomach from my eyes. Afterwards I put the dress back on and it moulds around my grotesque body.

The dress starts to smell. But I don't think any of my other clothes will fit. I'm seven stone four pounds. The highest I've been for a long time.

The days are still going by. Everyone's living, except me: I'm existing.

I venture from my bed. Mum has gone out to do the shopping. I only want to open my curtains to watch life go by.

There are fields and trees outside. It's still raining.

I walk towards the bedroom door and downstairs to the back door. I pull the handle down and it falls open. I glide down the path. The small stones cut through my bare feet.

The lock on the gate is stiff but I manage to pull it across. The gate opens.

I stand for a minute, overwhelmed with the sudden freedom I have. The rain is falling lightly onto me as if it knows I have come out for the first time in days and is being gentle to me.

I run: weaving in and out of the trees, running further away from home.

The gushing water bewitches my ears and I run towards the sound. The violent smashing of the current drags me to the scene.

Suddenly I stop.

I stand in the cutting water. Knives are being shoved into my legs and feet. It feels good.

The Alien is pleased with the pain.

I stare in front, at nothing. The water sploshes around me and I bend down towards it. I kneel on whatever exists on the bottom of this stream. The water comes to my waist. The dress parachutes out around me, freeing my legs to the loose stones that the current picks up and hurls at me.

I've never seen the stream with so much water in. It looks like a river. The violent gushing throws itself towards me and I push my arms under the water so that it comes to my neck.

My body looks murky. The rain starts to fall harder onto my head and I wonder whether I should put my head completely under.

"Die!" I start to whisper violently under my breath.

"Go away, leave me alone." I'm saying the words to no one.

I'm trying to help you, the Alien says. I can't argue. It's so powerful and logical that I know It speaks truth. It befriended me when I needed It. I cannot betray It now.

My head begins to sink on its own accord. I catch sight of a tree swaying in the wind. Its arms are bare and twisted.

My chin hits the cold water and the shock throws it back up. I can't take my eyes away from the tree. Against the force that tries to draw me under, I pull myself up.

I begin to walk up the hill, my dress sticking to me and dripping the water in a trail behind me. Through the undergrowth where dark, wet mud plasters my feet. I don't care what my feet step on as I walk to the gate that is swinging with the wind.

I feel oddly calm and relieved that I don't hear anything inside me. But I know It's gaining strength in this numb silence. I have to kill it while I have the chance. And to kill it means I must die. And I have the pills waiting for me in my room.

The house is still empty but it's as if I've been filled with new energy. My mind runs with thoughts.

I take off the dress which has turned brown with mud and I put on my night-dress. After tidying my things, I wash my hair to drain the mud away.

I feel calm and excited. My movements feel

slow and precise but also in staccato jolts. Everything has to be perfect. Tears are still falling but I'm not as upset. The drawer in my dressing table contains the answer.

I walk towards the kitchen where I pick up a drinking glass. I turn on the cold tap and fill it: the water gushing inside. I look up at the window and see Mum walking down the path. Her blue, knee-length skirt is blowing in the wind. I run upstairs sending some of the water slopping over the edge of the glass.

"Jasmine, I'm back!" she calls as the front door closes.

I don't reply.

Smiling to myself I put the glass down on the dressing table and then climb into bed. It's cold and I'm tired. My eyes close.

Eyes glare at me in the dream. Bulging eyes, Beth's eyes. Angels come floating to me from the sky, burning in bright colours. Then they turn to fires and a persistent smile shines through them. And I can hear a bell ringing loudly while the angel falls through the sky, getting closer to me.

Mum calls up to tell me dinner is ready. I drag myself out of bed and down the stairs to the table where the evil food sits.

I don't speak. I eat it all: the baked potato, the meat, the salad. I eat a slice of cake afterwards too - crumbling it with nerves, not with the usual thought of 'a broken biscuit leads to calorie leakage.'

After dinner I go to my room and close the door firmly behind me. I roll my desk-chair against it. My music is turned on loudly so that I can't hear any of the noises from the other side to distract me from my plan.

I pick up the box that contains the white painkillers. I pop them out from their holes. There's a pain so I'm sticking to the rules. The Alien inside is hurting me a lot and so the dosage will have to be increased to enable relief.

I know It's conning me but I do what I'm told and now I want the Alien to die. It seems the only way for this to happen is for me to die with It.

I put two tablets in my mouth and the glass to my lips. The water fills my mouth and the tablets begin to swim inside. I try to swallow. A white tablet, which I feel is fraying and disintegrating in the warmth and wet of its cage, won't go down.

If only I could make a similar prison for the Alien, it would die then. But I'm not allowed to think things like that.

The pill sits, lodged in my throat and it feels as if I have a snooker ball stuck there, choking me. I realise that I can't swallow twenty pills in case they all get stuck. So I drop pills into the glass of water. Each tablet makes little echoey sounds against the glass bottom.

I start to throw in any pill I can find: powdered Lemsips; soluble pills which hiss. I put the glass to my lips, my heart beating fast inside its prison. My mouth fills with the concoction. I swallow it quickly to take the disgusting taste away and I keep putting it to my lips. Again and again, allowing the liquid to seep down into my body.

I stop. I put the glass down and stare at it for a long time. Then I start again. Absorbing it in my body, allowing the venom to spread from my stomach and into my veins.

I don't think I've taken enough. The Alien is

angry with me. *You fool! You failure! Die, die.* And the word die is all that runs through my head as if someone tried photocopying the word but pressed the green button too many times. I have to do something else.

I see my dressing-gown belt hanging on a hook. I lift it off and tie it around my neck. Pulling it hard, my head starts to feel heavy and numb. Then a throb echoes inside. "Die" slows down and softens because it's obvious that I'm trying.

A force drags me to the floor. A similar force to the one which grabbed me in the stream. I still pull. My face feels huge and my head feels empty. Fluorescent raindrops fall in front of my eyes against the dark mist that has covered them.

The track on my CD player sings out. But I can't hear the words: only muffles reach my ears.

14

I wake in the morning and feel my head giving in to gravity. I look in the mirror and see that my eyelids are bulging as if they were the curtains on a stage that can't be wound all the way to the ceiling. My eyelashes seem to poke through the swelling. No matter how hard I try to open my eyes as wide as possible I can still see the swollen lids.

I try to put eye shadow on. Rimmel call the colour 'Orchid'. They don't look much better with it on. Is this what a lack of blood does to the head?

I have school but I don't want to go. I haven't told Mum. What am I going to do?

I look at my diary which lies on the floor. It's the only thing I can think of doing. I feel so attached to it.

Wednesday 14th April, Year 9.
Dear Diary,
  I don't know what happened. I've been dieting for about a year. Now my life is in ruins. I tried to kill myself yesterday. It's only because I feel so unhappy. Life is too hard. I HATE MYSELF. I eat too much and I feel so confused.

I was hoping I wouldn't wake up this morning, that I'd die in the night. But I woke up and I saw where I'd sat trying to strangle myself. All these horrible images came into my head; seeing myself there doing those things. I know it's awful but somehow I feel as if these torturous acts are justified because I deserve them.

Help me.

Love,

Jas xxx

"Mrs Corcoran, I can't tell her," I say at lunch.

Ade is with me. Her hair has been cut short into a bob. We talked at break and I told her that I had to find a way to stop everyone from finding out. I'd do anything.

"Anything?"

I nodded. "I did try anything," I said wondering if I should continue. "I tried to die."

She looked shocked. "How?"

"I'm sorry, I shouldn't have told you. I just wanted it all to go away. Let's forget it."

I didn't mean to tell her and I know the Alien is so angry with me.

Mrs Corcoran looks at me. "Well, I'll phone and we'll all meet up and talk about it."

Ade suddenly says, "Mrs Corcoran, there's something you should know."

"Yes," she says earnestly.

"I can't tell you." She looks at me. "It's for her to say."

"Are you going to tell me?" Mrs Corcoran asks, looking at me critically.

"I don't know what she's going on about," I say looking at her small face and despising every part of it. I notice her cheeks becoming slightly

114

redder than usual and she turns away from me as if she regrets telling her.

"Ok. I took some pills."

"How many?"

"I don't know."

"What, too many to count?"

"No, I put them in water. I just don't know." I'm giving up because I'm losing.

"Ok." She stops to think. "I'm going to contact your mum and you can come back at the beginning of lesson five."

"Do you want me to come with you," Ade asks when we leave the office.

I shrug. I can't talk to her anymore.

Mum's brown hair is left hanging down her back when she comes into school. Her under-skirt is slightly showing from under her tight, knee-length skirt. She wears no makeup.

We walk together up the steps, towards the office. Her heels click against the tiles and we neither of us say anything to each other.

We sit on the green seats.

"I've spoken to your mum on the phone," says Mrs Corcoran. "I'd like to leave the two of you in here to talk about things for a few minutes. Is that Ok with you, Jasmine?"

I nod. But it isn't.

The door closes.

"I've phoned Nurse Ratcliffe. She wants us to go to her clinic on Thursday and a doctor will talk to us."

I nod.

"You're going to have to start eating," she says.

"I'm sorry."

"So you'll forget this nonsense?"

"Yes."

We go to the appointment at Nurse Ratcliffe's clinic. I don't talk to Mum about food or dying and she doesn't ask. We drive in silence to the building where the nurse works. I've never seen it before, hidden away down a road I've never been to.

The doors are green and stiff to open. I pull them and we walk through. Nurse Ratcliffe is waiting for us and takes us to a little room. We all sit down.

"I'm going to weigh Jasmine," she says and I follow her to another room. It's like a cupboard. There are two scales and I stand on the ones she points at.

Red figures flash onto the dial. Forty-four kilograms. She writes it on the chart. I haven't put on any weight since the last time she weighed me. I feel relieved.

We go back to the room where Mum sits. Nurse Ratcliffe sits at the desk and gets the blue paper and a pencil. She draws something.

"You see this," she says holding out the paper to Mum, "this is her weight." She uses her pencil to show that I've lost a bit of weight since last time she weighed me. I feel ashamed. But the inside of me is pleased.

"Well, the doctor isn't quite ready to speak with you yet so would it be all right to go to the waiting room?"

We get up and walk to the waiting room.

I don't know the doctor's name. She comes to the door and calls me into the consulting room. I sit down, and she sits opposite me, at her desk.

There is a piece of paper in front of her and she fills it in as she asks me questions. They are stupid questions.

"Do you vomit?" she asks.

I shake my head.

"Why have you decided you want to lose weight?"

"I don't know."

The pen scribbles down notes onto the sheet of blue paper.

"Would you send your mum in now, please," she says.

I sit in the waiting room on my own. It's empty except for a few nurses who walk past. I read the posters on the wall to pass the time. There are ones about influenza and others about children.

I unzip my bag as quietly as I can. It's very quiet in the waiting room. I wonder where, or if, there are any patients. I clasp the camera I've brought and I put it up to my eye. I see the posters through the lens and click the button. The flash fills the room and then makes mechanical noises which sound deafening. I feel stupid and put it back in my bag.

Nurse Ratcliffe comes and talks to me. "Your hair looks nice today," she says. It is swinging from a ponytail.

"Thank you," I say.

The door opens and Mum comes out. She looks upset.

"She wants to see you again," she says.

I walk in and sit down. The doctor doesn't look happy.

"Did you try to kill yourself?" she asks.

I nod.

"Why didn't you tell me?"

"I don't know," I mumble.

"Why did you take the pills?"

"Because I didn't really want to tell my mum about me being on a diet."

"So how was that supposed to help?"

"I don't know," I say. What a stupid question. I'd be dead so I wouldn't have to tell anybody.

"I'm going to write a letter to Warings Hospital for an appointment with a different doctor."

Mum tells me I have an appointment at Warings Hospital with a doctor who's good with young people. It's taken them only a few days and I'm not sure how they managed to get me an appointment so quickly.

I thought I'd have time. Time to think and time to worry. But I have no time.

15

Warings hospital is a small building for outpatients. I wonder if this is a psychiatrist I'm seeing. I've heard about them. They are the ones mad people go and see. I'm only fourteen!

The floor is covered in maroon carpet, to hide the dirt, I bet. The chairs are covered with matching fabric. There aren't many empty ones. It's busy. Children are playing with the dolls house in the corner and people walking in and out of the door.

There's only one door into the rest of the building and it has a lock on it – no doubt to stop us mad patients from disturbing the peace inside.

It's as if the waiting room is full of disorder and the only treatment is to allow the patients to enter the internal area of the building. The only part that has a sane mind.

The doctors come and press the silver, numbered buttons to gain access. I try to watch, to master the code, but I can't see it clearly enough.

The door opens and a tall woman comes towards us. She kneels down in front of me. "Jasmine Harwood?"

"Yes that's her," Mum says.

"Would you like to follow me?"

We follow her.

Along the corridors and up the stairs. We enter a room and there are four seats. The carpet is still maroon and the chairs are still matching.

"I think Jasmine would rather talk to you on her own," Mum says. "Wouldn't you, Jas?"

I nod.

"Ok then I'll call you up later."

She goes.

"I'm Dr. Alphega," she says as she sits back down next to me.

She's wearing ankle boots, black lace ups and her skirt is green. The skirt almost meets the tops of the boots. I can't help thinking how strangely normal it is in this surreal situation. It makes me smile to think about it.

"Do you know why you're here?" she asks. She turns in her chair and looks at me kindly, unthreateningly. I see her diamond stud earrings twinkling at me. I wonder if they're real diamonds.

"Yeah," I mumble. "I went on a diet and tried to kill myself." Why is she asking me? Doesn't she know?

She's nicer than the doctor I saw before, whose name I don't remember.

"Do you cry a lot?" she asks.

I nod.

I'm scared and I can feel all the nerves inside my stomach jumping around as if they're the atoms of liquid being heated and coming to the boil over a Bunsen burner.

Mum comes up to the room so that Dr Alphega can speak to both of us.

"Well, Jasmine is suffering from depression. I

would like to put her on a course of antidepressants." She looks over at me and smiles.

I look at mum scared that she will tell me off.

"And I'd like to see her twice a week." She gives Mum the prescription form. I want to say that I'd heard children couldn't get depressed but I don't. I must be wrong.

I've forgiven Ade. I just won't trust her again. She comes to my house to stay the night. I hide the photos I've had developed because she'll think they're weird. The ones at the clinic have been done and it's really strange to see it because it's not how I remember it. The photos contain the truth but not the truth in my memory. Besides, posters about influenza really are quite boring.

I need to get my motivation back and start taking more pictures. I want to take atmospheric ones but I know that I need to practice.

Ade and I walk on the valley as the sun is setting. A perfect photo scene. It's still cold and we wear our coats to protect us from the April coldness.

"What is it they say, 'Red sky at night is Turkish deli'"

"*Shepherds'* delight!" she says, laughing.

We sit down on the grass and stare at the sky.

"Angel delight and Turkish delight. Mmmm, food," I say.

"Someone sounds hungry," she says looking at me.

"No, I was just commenting on the sky!"

"Why didn't you tell someone about all of this food stuff before?"

"I don't know," I say.

Once the alien feeling was established I could not loosen Its grip on me. Asking for help, or even telling someone that there was so much pain, was impossible.

"So then, tell me about your love-life," she says.

I don't care about anything like that. I just want to lose weight, but if I tell her that she'll think I'm not normal.

"I haven't really had a boyfriend," I say. "I really fancied this boy called Nathan but I don't anymore. Cori used to tease me about it all the time."

"So you've never kissed a boy?"

"Well, have you?"

"Yes!" she laughs.

"Properly?"

She looks at me as if it's a stupid question. Then she smiles, "Ok, so it was only a peck on the cheek!"

We giggle.

"But don't worry," she adds, "I'll sort you out with a nice lad."

I lie down and stare at the sky again.

The sky has turned to a darker shade of red and the clouds swim across in colours just as dark. I wonder if Cori has come from heaven or hell.

"Are you religious?" I ask suddenly.

"Na. You?"

"Not really. I was brought up Church of England, but that was because of Dad and he's dead now so we don't bother."

"Cori said your dad isn't dead."

"She's funny about my dad. He died when I

was born. I think she lies about it because her dad had a nervous breakdown last year."

"How did he die?"

"I don't want to talk about it."

"Sorry. I'll change the subject. So how do you think we got here?"

"Don't go all philosophical on me," I say.

"Ok."

I can hear the rushing of the stream I had run into. It sounds as if it's still full of water.

I look at her. Her brown eyes look distant.

"My father set fire to our house when I was 10," she says.

"Oh my word! Why? Were you hurt?"

"No. We weren't hurt. Don't know why he did it although I think he was drunk but that's only a guess. I think he's not all there in the head." She rolls her eyes and sighs.

She has a screwed up family so she would have a reason to do what I do. I have no reason. I am guilt-ridden.

We neither of us say anything else. It's as if there aren't any words to describe feelings or thoughts.

The sun creeps away from sight and at the edge of the horizon a beautiful array of colours spread across the sky. The colours echo as if they're from the glass school. And then they slowly disappear.

We silently lie side by side until the darkness floods around us and we go home.

Part Three

Echoes

16

"Hello, Jasmine. Come in and sit yourself down," Nurse Ratcliffe says.

I sit on the plastic chair.

"How are you?" she asks.

"Ok thanks."

"Good. Well I have this for you." She opens my file and carries on talking. "The dietician looked at your food diary. I'm sorry it took so long. Here's the verdict." She places the printed slip in front of me.

"Right," she says, "your diet should comprise of thirty-five percent fat. You have forty-five percent. You should have fifty percent carbohydrate, you have forty-two percent. And you should have fifteen percent protein, you have eleven."

I stare at the paper and hate it. The roots of the Alien have been fed as they grab hold of her words to constantly remind me how much I need to lose weight.

"So you're not eating enough," she says. "We could probably do with cutting back on the amount of fat. Anyway we can think about that.

How's it going with Dr Alphega?"

"Ok," I say.

"What has she said?"

"I'm on medication."

"Do you know what it's called?"

I shake my head.

"Have you noticed any changes?"

I shake my head again.

I sit at the top of the stairs each Tuesday and Thursday morning.

"I'm not going," I say.

"Well, you've got up now and you're dressed so you might as well go," Mum says.

I walk slowly down each step. My heart pounds fast and the Alien screams at me so that I can't hear anything. Flashing lights are in my eyes so that I can't see properly. I walk to the front door and talk to myself, "I'm not going," I say. "I'm only pretending. I'm fooling them really." But the Alien knows I'm lying.

My heart scrapes my inside each time it beats so that it hurts every second we get nearer to Warings Hospital.

The building appears at the side of the road. The car pulls into the car park. No matter how hard I try there's no getting out of it.

Dr Alphega comes to the door and I walk towards her. We go to her room and sit in the usual places, me on the left by the desk and her next to me, on the right.

I don't speak. I can't. I look at the floor. It makes patterns at me flying and merging into vivid lights that never die. They wait here to torment me. The more they dance the dizzier I get. I can't make them go away and I'm scared they will make me faint.

I look at the two empty chairs opposite. One has scratches on the left wooden leg: three small scratches, to be exact.

Either the cleaner or Dr Alphega has been moving the chairs because they all seem further apart. Thank goodness.

I rest my eyes on the chair and the patterns stop dancing. I can hear her voice but I can't understand it. I feel as if I am dreaming. Am I? Am I really here?

Her voice stops and there is complete silence. I don't like the silence in her room. I'm scared hunger will explode disturbing this silence. Usually I like it, but not here, not with her.

Sometimes I forget she's there and I drift. I catch the odd word that flies towards me. She talks about a bad part and that she hopes to make me feel less alone and to make the good part stronger. But she seems to add to the confusion so I don't listen.

I move my arm very suddenly. It just happens without me controlling it. I stop drifting and feel so stupid for allowing it to happen so obviously.

I look towards the door and wonder how much longer I have to wait. I feel my face burning. Why couldn't a muscle in my face have twitched rather than the whole of my arm? I hate this. I really do. The Alien is laughing at me. I drop my head and my hair falls forward and I start to mutter quietly.

"You're so stupid," I say to myself, "stupid," and I dig my nails into the skin of my fingers as hard as I possibly can.

"Well, I'm afraid our time is up. I'll just write down some more appointments for you." She picks up her black diary from the floor where she keeps all her documents. She turns pages and writes down my twice-weekly appointments on the white paper. I look at my fingers and see the dents of half-moons.

I'm relieved it is over even though I know it won't be long before I am there again.

I can't go to school now. After my appointments I can't do anything but sit on the sofa and stare at nothing. When Mum goes to work I curl up and cry. Why won't the thing inside stop hurting me? Why won't It die?

I sit at my desk and pull out some paper. I hold a pencil and stare at the whiteness. Somehow the white, bare paper seems scary.

I start to draw a head. I make the eyes go cross-eyed and a nose like a pig. I draw a knife flying into the head at the ears. Steam comes from the nose, blood pouring out of the ears.

On her forehead I write, 'stupid child' because that is what Dr Alphega thinks when I am there.

I smile when I look at it because it looks a little like her. I add it to the folder which contains a copy of my food diary and the pages of 'I am fat.'

I think I can hear the Alien chuckling from deep inside. Just a moment of relief before It is shocked by the amount of fat that sits on my body.

I walk to the scales. I'm almost crying before I know what I weigh. The dial spins. "Please let me weigh no more than seven stones," I beg to whoever can control the scales.

Seven stone two pounds.

Look at this! It says in absolute disgust.

"I know," I say with the tears streaming down

my cheeks.

I warned you that if you didn't do what I said you'd feel horrible.

"But I already feel horrible," I say.

You have to lose weight. You're eating too much. Sort it out. Get down to seven stone first and then we'll think about what to do. But you have to do something because you're ugly and fat.

I go back to my desk and start to make plans for my diet with real vigour. There is no turning back and there are no options. I either lose weight or I die.

I cannot live with this tormenting me when I'm overweight. I know I will be so much happier when I'm thin.

I get some more white plain paper to write the pros and cons of listening to the Alien.

Advantages from listening

You can be thin
You won't have fat legs
You can wear nice clothes
You don't have to have a horrible taste of chocolate in your mouth
You won't be worrying about being a chocoholic because there'll be no chance!
You can relax and have more confidence in yourself
You'll be so much healthier than anyone else when you cut out all that fat.

Disadvantages from listening

People say you're thin but you still think you're fat
You cry after you eat because you'll get fatter
People tell you you'll end up in hospital (but you know it's just a healthy diet)
People really get on your nerves telling you you're only doing it for attention and then fall out with you
It's hard to stick to a diet
People really hate you
You worry about what you eat

I look at the two sheets of paper and decide that I have to diet. I call it my Miracle Diet because I will lose weight. I write down rules so that I don't lose any determination. The Alien writes them for me. I barely have to think about what I'm writing.

RULES:

* *Eat as little as possible. Don't you dare eat more than you can get away with*
* *Your first target weight is seven stone. Your next is six stone seven pounds. The last is six stone four pounds. You should be thin by then*

I'm not thinking at all. I can't hear Its voice clearly.
I just know the Alien has taken over because I feel the pain of what I weigh.
I carry on writing. I'll feel calmer when I know

what I'm doing.

- *Do not give up. Remember life will be great when you're gorgeous, when you're thin*
- *When the urge to eat comes then remember to say, one, two, three, thin, thin, thin!*
- *At six forty-five in the morning do fifty sit-ups. Increase this number if you stop losing weight*
- *Stamp your foot each morning three times while repeating the word 'thin'*
- *Always exercise. No less than one and a half hours a day*
- *Talk as little as possible – you need no friends. They only hurt you*
- *Talk to no one about dieting*

I smile when I finish because I feel secure. I fold my arms across my chest. "You see," I say out loud, "I'll get thin if it's the last thing I do."

And how long have you been saying that? It asks.

"For over a year but I'll do it this time."

17

Another appointment, another Thursday. The Alien screams at me because It hates me going to see her.

I decide that today I will tell her to stop telling me about the Bad Part that wants me to die. I'll tell her that this so called Bad Part tries to help me and keeps me alive. I'll take my sunglasses. They'll protect me from the room.

I use my fountain pen to write the note for Dr Alphega:

This 'bad part' you describe isn't bad because it's trying to help me. No one else has ever bothered to help me and look after me.

When she comes to the door I walk over to her and pull my sunglasses out of my bag. I unfold them and slide them onto my face. Everything turns to a darker shade.

We sit down and silence fills the room.

I hand her the note.

"Thank you," she says. She looks at it briefly and then says, "This is very helpful." She pauses for a moment. "Yes, I can see that you would feel it wants to help you. But there is a small part of you that's desperate to get away from this part, to reach out and to be made stronger. That's the Good Part of you that I need to strengthen."

She's missing the point.

I sit feeling pleased. I haven't broken the rule of silence. But I won't eat today, just in case It's angry with me for confessing Its existence to the outside world.

She seems to be thinking because she then says, "Can you tell me about your father?"

I freeze. I daren't move or breathe. Why does she want to know?

The silence creeps over us as the time ticks.

"Perhaps you could tell me about your father next time. You could write it down if you'd like to."

School feels as if it's a surreal place where strange objects move from room to room. I join in the movements but I don't make the same sounds as them. I sit at desks, red ones which once had waves pushing the paper Cori had torn along the top. I watch the girls talk.

"Look how short her skirt is!"

"Oh it's not really that short. My mum would kill me if she knew what I did to it."

The girl demonstrates how she makes her skirt short. She lets it fall to its full length, just below the knees. She rolls the waistband over and over so that the skirt becomes shorter.

She giggles as she shows her audience. "I have to watch that it doesn't sag round my backside," she says. They laugh.

She turns around when the teacher comes in and I see the material has gathered around her bum. I snigger to myself, but I don't really find it funny. I don't care. Perhaps I would have once but things have changed. These little things don't really matter.

Beth has decided she's had enough of me. I don't care. Ade and her are best friends now. We hardly ever speak, but always seem to be watching each other.

I look over at Cori. She's with Beth and Ade and they're laughing. She sees me watching and I turn my head away.

"You all right, Jasmine?" she says, calling over to me.

I nod.

I start to dream like I did before the suicide attempt.

I dream of being thin. I look at my right wrist. I like my wrists because they're the thinnest part of me. I feel the round bone at the right side and how it carves itself into the rest of the hand. I see the blue veins, crossing over each other and making roads to different destinations. The roads which carry blood. I like the hollow on the left side. It has a road traveling through it too.

I stop looking at my wrist because I have no reason to be proud. I have a long way to go before I am there, before I reach thinness.

I see the fine hairs of eyebrows burrowing towards each other and a familiar shine. Cori stands in front of me as if she were a goddess.

"Wake up, Girl." She starts to laugh her horrid laugh. She stops. "Missing your friends? Ha! You have no friends."

She leans towards me and whispers, "I told you you'd have no friends. I'm always right." She lifts her head away from mine and smiles smugly to herself. She looks at me as if she has finished a piece of Artwork that she is proud of. She is proud of my loneliness, my nothingness.

I look at her. "What do you want?"

"I came to get you back from Never Never Land. We wouldn't want you not growing up, now would we?" She leans towards me on the red table. She laughs in my face. "Besides we have an agreement."

Is she talking about her threat of death? My world of solitude isn't enough for her.

"Just leave me alone," I say and try to ignore all her words.

I pull out my notebook and roll pages over the wires at the top until I get a free page. My fountain pen feels heavy as I write.

I write to myself all the time. I write on any scrap pieces of paper that I can find and even on my exercise books. *If you don't feel dizzy, if you can't feel bone then you're fat no matter what others say. Feeling ill when you're on a diet is what you're supposed to feel and soon you'll love it. Believe me.*

I have to scribble out the words on the lined pages of my schoolbooks, and tear pages out of my notebook to file so that people won't find them.

I close my notebook and look around me. I catch Cori still looking at me. She smiles. I don't.

"Jasmine, come downstairs a minute," Mum calls.

But I'm not supposed to leave Never Never land. That's where Cori thinks I live. I'll have to be quick. I'll time it. I walk slowly to the door. As soon as it opens I run down and into the kitchen where Mum stands trying to put her hand into the hole of her black coat.

"What?" I say harshly.

"I'm going shopping after work." She stops and watches me tap my foot.

"What are you doing?" she asks.

"Will you get on with it?" I shout. "I've got to go back." I look at my watch. "Damn," I say.

"What?"

"It's too late now. I have to go upstairs." I run up the stairs before the air in the house contaminates me.

I hear her sigh as I run up. She doesn't say anything else to me and she doesn't follow.

Wednesday 5th May, Year 9.
Dear Diary,

Mum hates me. I know she does. There used to be people in my life. There's only me now. I am alone with the Alien inside me. It still grows roots, soaks up peoples' harsh comments as if it's the water It needs to feed off.

Diary, even school is full of torment for me that echoes around the windowed corridors.

Until I reach my goal of thinness I have to exist in this lonely, non-existent world, where everyone is fighting a battle against me.

Love
Jas xxx

I wonder what Dr Alphega thinks about me believing that her interpretation of the Alien is wrong and that really it's actually the Good Part. I hope she's lost and that she can't cope with the way I complicate things. I feel ok thinking that.

I feel the Alien inside getting uncomfortable when I think of Dr Alphega. It says, *You're just part of her work and a case to her. She hates you because you make her job harder. She could never really care. It's all a pretence.*

"I know," I say. "She doesn't like me at all." I see the picture I'd drawn of her in my head. "Why is it I am expected to talk about all of my feelings to someone who I don't even know?"

Because she gets paid for it! the Alien says.

I pull the quilt over my head and hear my stomach exploding with hunger. I touch it and feel the hollow between my hip bones which stick out like two volcanoes. I look at my stomach and see a pulse beating inside it. It's as if my heart has fallen. I smile and close my eyes, waiting for sleep - but it never does come.

I come out from under my quilt and take some paper off my bedside table.

What is there to tell Dr Alphega about my dad? What does she want to know? The white of the paper looms up at me. I pick up a pencil because it can't ever be permanent.

My Dad's dead.

I get out of bed, fold the paper and put it neatly into my school bag. I leave my bedroom, where it is the safest place to exist, and emerge into the battleground. My only protection is my pair of sunglasses.

I pass the note to Dr Alphega as soon as she has sat down.

"Thank you," she says as she unfolds the paper. I hear it crackling open.

"This is very helpful. Thank you for writing this." She stops, as she always does, gathering thoughts and words inside her head. "I'm so sorry it seems as if your father is dead."

Why only seem? She doesn't believe a word I write. No wonder my words are useless.

"I've been thinking about the different parts to you," she says, her diamond earrings glinting. "All of us have different parts in us, a good part and a bad part. But for some people that Bad Part takes control of them and becomes too strong." She stops as if I am supposed to say something. Maybe I am meant to agree or argue.

I am silent

"My job is to find a way to help you. Everyone's different, just the way that identical twins aren't genetically identical. Illnesses are similar enough to put into categories but even then they aren't identical."

I wonder what she's saying it for and I start to feel strange as if I'm losing this. "I don't want to change," I say, suddenly thinking that's what she's hinting at.

"Change is scary. I'm here to make you feel less alone."

I sit holding my breath. I let it go and feel too scared to take in any more for a moment.

"I need to protect you against this destructive force. You're being told you mustn't have friends and mustn't trust anybody. The bad part that you describe has given you the impression of safety. But it lies to you."

I still stare and pretend not to listen but I am attentive to every word she forms.

"Perhaps we can look at this in a similar way. I'm feeding the Good Part so that it will become strong enough to fight and kill this other growth. It'll be like our sessions here is the only source of life to encourage the good part to grow. But eventually there will be other external factors that will encourage its growth too."

I look at the carpet and the patterns dance at

me. The glasses make them dingy. They protect the only entrance to the inside of me.

"Tell me about school."

I say nothing.

She takes a piece of paper and a pen from beside her chair and passes them to me.

"Just write any words that come into your head. Anything that resembles your present life at school or your past experiences of school."

I hold the paper that she's given me. The crinkles of the paper are deafening.

I write words:

Girls. Nastiness. Glass. Colours. Noise. Death.

And underneath the words I write sentences:

They spread rumours and echo them in the glass corridors of the school. They threaten me with death. I don't hear their words anymore. There's just noise that merges with colours that are so bright now.

I turn away as she reads it.

"I'm so sorry that school is like this. It sounds so awful. School is meant to be a place to learn not where people are nasty to you and threaten to kill you."

The patterns become fierce, jumping up at me. I almost push back in my chair they come so close. It's as if they're going to swallow me up.

I know why they've become so vivid: she's trying to kill the Alien. But the Alien has so faithfully helped me through these years and is doing this one last thing for me. I must not let her kill It.

I see her in a burning building. She's calling for help, trying to hold out her hands so that I can catch them. "I tried to help you, now help me!" she shouts.

I am motionless. Then I begin to laugh. I can't stop. I fall onto the floor and carry on laughing. The flames jump up around her, chewing her and loving her and then swallowing her.

"Do you keep a diary?" Her words cut through my vision.

I nod.

"Have you kept one from when you first started senior school?"

I nod.

"Would you be able to tell me bits about your diary when we next meet?"

I don't know how to respond. I want to say yes. I feel I need to say no.

I shrug.

"Well, have a think about it and we can talk about the diary together at our next appointment."

Just as I get up from my chair she says, "Oh, before I forget, I was thinking I may wear my sunglasses next time we meet."

I stand very still. What does she want me to say to that? She always confuses me so I carry on walking towards the door and ignore it.

18

"I hate going to Warings," I say to Nurse Ratcliffe.

"But it's the best thing for you at the moment."

"But I hate it so much." I've never said so much to her in my life.

"Well, why don't you tell her?"

"I can't talk to her." And I know that I shouldn't be talking to her either. But I'll try anything to get me out of seeing Dr Alphega.

"OK, let's think about what makes it so difficult. Can you tell me?"

"I just hate it." I stare at the floor.

I've said enough.

"Well, have a think about it and see if you can tell me what is so bad next time we meet."

I do think about it. I sit in my room, in silence. I'm not moving, just staring at my watch. Five minutes has gone by but I will sit here for a whole twenty minutes. There is no choice. I need to discover what it is that makes me hate being at Warings hospital so much.

The twenty minutes pass sluggishly. I don't know why I hate it. There are no answers.

What is it that's so terrible about sitting here

in silence? Nothing.

I'll have to sit for another twenty minutes to see if this one will tell me what I need to know. There has to be a way of finding out what's so terrible.

Suddenly I feel a gnawing hunger.

I wish there were chains and locks across the kitchen cupboards. I shouldn't be eating anything. The scales show that I weigh too much. Too, too much.

Six stone eleven pounds did please me two days ago. But I feel bored by it now. What am I doing so wrong that makes it stay static?

The initial pleasure turns to disgust. The number is so far from my goal.

I open the cupboard door and the chocolate biscuits stare out at me, enticing me.

Perhaps I could chew them and then spit them out. It would be ok then. I take the packet to my room holding an empty glass and a pile of tissues in my other hand.

Once I'm sitting on my chair I carefully and slowly unwrap the biscuits. The first biscuit peeks out. It's upside down but I can still smell the chocolate filling my nose and tempting me to sin.

I hold the biscuit in my hand for a second. This is the moment when I have not yet sinned but am contemplating the terrible action. I slowly place it in my mouth chewing it carefully and slowly. Putting the glass to my lips I use my tongue to push out the brown, warm biscuit.

The white tissues become stained as I wipe them across my mouth. I look at the other biscuits in the packet, sleeping. I put another inside my mouth and chew but the muscles in my throat insist on swallowing. I feel the warm mound slide down my throat.

Ecstasy. I can't stop now. I must finish the packet.

The packet is empty.

The scales say seven stone. My school skirt feels tight around my waist. What am I going to do?

I sit at my desk and put my head in my hands. Perhaps I should kill myself. I feel so much pain that anything seems better than this.

I pick up my black biro and write:

I hope someday you'll understand and accept my death. I don't know why or when it started but the mental torment is killing me. I know I don't look anorexic as I'm not emaciated but there are many things you don't know and will never understand.

I even avoid school because I can't face it when I am looking so huge. I can't bear anyone looking at me because I see them looking at my fat and laughing at my ugliness...

I give up trying to explain. There are no words to describe such pain.

"So have you thought about why you don't like going to Warings Hospital?" Nurse Ratcliffe asks.

"I've thought so hard," I say, "but I honestly don't know."

"Well, at least you've given it some thought. It's something we can work on. Anyway, how are you?"

"Ok," I say.

"You look a bit down."

I look at my hands. I say nothing.

"Are you?"

I shrug. Fat is all that I can think of.

"Are you sleeping?"

I shrug.

"Jasmine I need you to listen."

I listen because her tone is hard and even. I'm in trouble.

"I'd like to weigh you."

"No," I say almost shouting.

She looks quite surprised. Even I'm shocked by my outburst.

I don't stop, I can't. *Don't let her. Don't let her. Don't let her,* is all that I can hear in my head.

"You're never going to weigh me again." I try to move my feet and walk out. My dramatic exit.

It fails. My legs won't move.

"Jasmine, I have to weigh you every now and again. I've been asked to do this. I don't want to make this hard for you but I do have to weigh you. You don't have to look. You could stand on them backwards."

I sit silently. She stands up and walks over to the scales.

I stand.

"Take off your shoes and cardigan."

I take off my shoes, positioning them neatly by the side of the table as I always did the times before. I do not take off my cardigan. She looks at me but I refuse to give her everything she's asking for.

I stand on the murky brown square. The horror-machine that has the nurse as its witness. A witness to my failure.

The horrid numbers spin past and I hear them making the horrible noise. The Alien hates me. I can feel roots like those of strong trees. The roots are so powerful, bursting through paving stones, and grass. It feels like I'm in their way and they will burst through me too. *Failure!*

Cori was nothing compared to my own torment. She was just preparing me for the real test.

"Ok," the nurse says.

I quickly look down and see that I am forty-five kilograms. How I hate her scales.

After each appointment at Warings I detest it more. The lull of the road as the early morning sun shines down does not calm me.

I have my diary in my bag. My comfort, my friend. Now my betrayer.

"Dad sent you a letter this morning," Mum says as she turns the last left before we arrive there. "He's sent you some money."

"I don't want any money from him."

"I think you might want this. It's a lot." She pauses a little and pushes her hair behind her ear. "It's three hundred pounds."

I say nothing.

It would be nice to have three hundred pounds. I could buy so many things. I could buy clothes, some electronic scales. I could have some fun.

"No, I don't want the money."

She says no more as she maneuvers the car into the last space available in the small car park.

I look at the other cars already parked. Some are new and expensive looking. Others are older. I wonder which car Dr Alphega drives. Maybe one of the newer looking posh cars to keep up with an expensive life-style.

We wait together on the maroon chairs. Although we sit side by side we are separated by silence.

The door opens and Dr Alphega stands while I walk towards the door. I follow her through the corridors. I count the stairs as I mount them. Once at the top I pull my sunglasses from my coat pocket and place them on my face.

I have nothing to say once I am in the room. I have nothing to say to anybody. I shall exist in silence.

She unfolds her sunglasses and puts them over her eyes. "I know it's hard for you to talk but it's important that we meet."

We both sit with our sunglasses and I feel stupid.

It's as if we sit amongst graves on bitty grass against Yew trees.

I dream.

Dad is buried beneath my feet and I sit by the side of his grave. The stone is missing, just a space where it should be. The grass is wet, but I don't mind. I stare at the emptiness of where the stone used to stand.

My feet start to sink through the wet grass as if they're trying to suck me under the ground to where he lies. Crows dance together in the sky, the only things making any noise. The ground starts to swallow my legs and the sun sinks through the sky as if escaping from England.

"Jasmine, I want to make these bad feelings go away," she says.

I want to shout, "Well make this stop then. It's happening right here in front of you and you do nothing." But I sit and dig my nails as hard as possible into my hand. Does she notice?

Tears begin to drip down my face, past the black frames of the glasses. My hair conceals each tear from her.

I'm trapped in an unreal world where nobody can reach me.

19

Why doesn't Dr Alphega see my pain? I take my diary to each appointment in the hope that she can magically feel the pain through the words that I write inside the pages.

"The words you wrote about school," she says, "they're very interesting." She stops and sits silently.

I try to breathe evenly to make the panic I feel crawling up into my lungs subside.

"The words are very emotive. The echoes and the glass particularly make me wonder about school. Are you able to tell me more."

The rule of silence, is all I keep thinking.

I stretch my arm to my bag that sits beside my chair.

I open my mouth to speak. Nothing falls out.

"Is that your diary?" she asks.

I nod.

I flick through a few pages until something looks interesting. I'm not really thinking, I'm too conscious of being seen.

I stop at a page.

"Would you be able to read me some bits from it?" she asks.

"I'll try." My words are so quiet I see her stretching out trying to reach them with her ears.

"This is an entry that I wrote in the summer, before I started Year 9."

I can't believe I'm saying so much. This is wrong. This is terrible. I feel I have betrayed myself.

"I'll just read fragments...

Cori hates me. She has everyone on her side. They echo words in the glass school that bounce straight to my ears. She told me she's going to kill me. I am still waiting. I wish she'd hurry up. The pain is so bad now."

I can't read more. It's embarrassing. The tears are behind my sunglasses again.

"It sounds so terrible," she says. "I'm so sorry that this is what you are subjected to when you go into school. Do you have any other friends?"

"Well, there's Beth and Ade. I suppose."

"Can you stay with them and keep away from Cori?"

"They're all interconnected... It's just really complicated. But I spose I could try."

"Yes, if you can try then that's something."

Familiar silence lives and breathes in the room. Too much has been spoken here. Now it's being purged.

I sit in maths with my hand hovering over my calculator. The sun is streaming through the windows and we've all taken off our cardigans. I see the fat on my arms and know that the other girls in the class will also see it.

"Are you all right?" Beth asks as she walks back to her desk from the front.

I nod. She looks at me briefly but then goes back to her desk with Cori.

Cori looks over at me. "So then, Jas, what's it

like being on the other side of sanity?"

Beth laughs nervously with her. I see the fear in Beth's face that was there when she was Cori's friend before. It's like she doesn't quite know what to expect. Her bulging eyes dart around as if on the lookout for danger. Every now and again her delicate voice swims to my ears but I don't hear the words. I put my head on the table and close my eyes.

The doorbell rings and I hear mum answer it.

"Oh!" I hear her say.

I walk to my bedroom door and open it quietly so that no one can hear me listening.

"Yes, she's upstairs. She's not well, you know."

"Really?" a man's voice says, "She got a bug?"

"No, no. Not as simple. She's anorexic."

My heart spins and my head sinks. A pain I've never felt to such intensity before screams and shoves knives into me. Those words she said, they do not belong to me. They are not me. I'm too fat to be anorexic. I am still a person, even if a little weird.

"Can I see her?" the man persists.

"Well..."

"Did you get the letter and money I sent?"

And like a ton of bricks falling over me I know it's Dad. Why does the stranger have to come back?

I scream and scream. "Don't let him in Mum. NO! NO! NO!"

I slam my bedroom door shut and crouch on the floor in front of it.

I scream so loudly that it hurts my ears. I wonder if someone will call an ambulance. I'm so confused that I can't think. My head falls into my hands while my thoughts merge into a tangled ball of wool.

There are so many tears that I can't see anything. I can't breathe. "He's not my dad. He's not. He's dead."

I gasp for air because the tightness in my chest is still there. I'm weak from the tears that have fallen and the screaming that I've screamed.

Silence.

I hear no siren. No one has called the police to lock me away. But neither has anyone come to me. Is there anyone here?

Why have I been abandoned? Again?

I turn the tap on in the bathroom and splash my face with cold water. Then I slowly walk downstairs.

Mum sits in the living room watching the news.

She sees me at the door and turns the sound down. "You'll have to see him, Jas. He's your dad."

"Only when he wants to be."

"Ok, so he's not the most reliable man on earth. But he's here now."

"He's the one who left."

She sighs. "Well, I told him you'd phone."

"Never," I say.

I leave her there because I don't want to argue anymore.

I close my bedroom door and crouch in front of it. No one ever seems to listen to me or take me into account.

My hifi system sits silently in the corner and I'm tempted to put on a CD. But the silence seems to surround me and I can't break out of it.

My diary beckons me, my only friend. I open it and begin to write an entry.

Thursday 15th June, Year 9.
Dear Diary
You won't believe what has happened to me today. Dad turned up. It's like a resurrection, an indestructible figure returning from the dead. He stood there (I assume because I didn't see him) and talked to Mum like nothing had ever happened.

I can't believe it. I swore I would never see him and here he is asking to see me.

Mum said I'd phone, but there's no way on this earth that I'd do that. And that's final.
Love
Jas xxx

20

Nurse Ratcliffe smiles at me as I walk towards her. I don't know why she's not in her office, sitting at her desk waiting for me.

"Hello Jasmine," she says warmly.

I try very hard to return her smile.

We walk into the room and I sit down.

"So how are we doing?"

"Ok," I say.

"Still seeing Dr Alphega?"

I nod.

"Still taking the medication?"

I nod.

"Have you noticed anything yet?"

I shake my head.

She opens the file she has on her desk. It's brimming with paper: notes about me, letters from people and to people.

"Well," she says checking the information before continuing, "it does take some time before they start to work." She smiles. "Also, if they don't work then there are others that you could try. It's something I can talk to Dr Alphega about. With your permission, of course."

She stops speaking. And we neither of us say anything.

"Would that be ok if I were to speak to her?"
she says.

I nod.

She closes the file.

"So then what have you been up to recently?"

My mind goes blank and all I can think is
that Dad's not dead. Dad is not dead.

"Um," I say, "well," I look at the opposite end
of the room and notice how the silver filing
cabinet has chunks of silver scratched away. "My
Dad's not dead," I say.

Where did the words come from? I heard
them in the open but I didn't feel myself speaking
them.

"I didn't think your dad was dead."

"Oh, sorry. No. He wasn't. I just meant to say
he's come back."

She nods. "Where has he been all this time?"

"I don't know."

"How do you feel about it?"

I think about the question but feel nothing
that I can put into words.

"I don't know," I say, feeling stupid.

"Did you speak to him?"

I shake my head.

"Are you going to?"

"If my Mum gets her way."

She laughs. "You seem to always see
everything as a battle."

Everything is a battle. It's pointless to tell her
this.

She looks at her watch, "I'm going to have to
go now, Jasmine. I need to be at another school
to give some injections. But I'd like to see you
again soon and maybe we can talk some more
about this."

I say nothing.

"If you'd like to," she says.

"I don't mind," I say.

I leave the room and walk down the corridor to my next lesson. I know the route there well and could almost do it with my eyes closed if it weren't for all the girls walking around, obstructing my way.

There are still girls in the classroom eating their lunch and so I lean against the wall and drop my bag on the floor. I look out of the window opposite and see the trees at the side of the school. Those trees will still be here next week. They will stand there blowing in the wind whether I see my Dad or not. Somehow I don't seem important.

Cori walks through the doors at the end of the corridor. She's with Ione. "What you doing here, Moron?"

"What does it look like I'm doing? Waiting for the bell to go so that I can go in for my lesson."

Ione looks at Cori. Cori has her big lipstick smile. Her mouth parts to release a bubble of giggles.

I roll my eyes just as they look at me. Too late, they've seen.

"Oh my word, Jas! You must be so thick to be in this set! We're in set 1 for Geography. We have brains."

"Whatever," I say wishing and willing them to go.

I wonder if I have time to walk away. Where are the nearest toilets? Or would they just follow me?

"Corisande!" Mrs Dorrian says as she walks towards us.

I try to smile at her. She doesn't look my way.

"Cori could you do me a favour? I need you to show some parents round the school. I know I can trust you to do a sensible job."

Cori smiles sweetly. "Of course I can."

"You'll have to miss your afternoon lessons but I'll speak to your teachers to let them know. Of course this will be recorded in your report too." She smiles a huge smile and then she takes Cori through the corridor.

Ione stands with me.

She silently looks me up and down. Her face is expressionless. And then she says, "All right for some."

"Yeah," I mumble. Are we pretending to be friends for a short moment?

Without another word she silently glides away.

The bell rings. The classroom purges itself of people.

I pick up my bag and walk in. I choose my usual seat at the back where Beth will come and join me. Dr Alphega wants me to be friends with Beth and Ade. I must try.

There are several girls giggling by the lockers, not wanting to leave for their lessons. The blackboard is covered in rude words and cartoon drawings of teachers.

The chair scrapes against the floor as I pull it out.

"Hi Jas," Beth says as she walks in. "Just saw Cori being a guide for the parents."

"Mrs Dorrian asked her to do it. Being teachers pet and all."

"Yeah, along with her sister too."

"Ione wasn't asked to do it."

"Well, she's some how wangled her way in."

"Typical. Those two are never apart."

"Joined at the hip."

"Nah, joined at the brain. They don't know who they are when they're not together."

"That's true," she says slapping her exercise books against the table.

She sits down next to me. I look at her and see her china face, so delicate.

"Whoa, it's hot in here," she says. "It's all these windows letting in the sun."

I can feel the sun through my large stitched cardigan. My back absorbs every fragment of sun and spreads warmth through me.

"How can you sit there with your cardie on in this heat?" she says taking hers off.

I laugh. "Oh I'm not that hot," I say even though I feel myself getting hotter.

She shrugs and gets her pencil case out. She finds her red pen and writes on the last page of the exercise book *Beth 4 Andrew.*

"Oooh," I say snatching the book out from beneath her hands and holding it up. "A boyfriend?"

"No!" She blushes and smiles. "But I wish," and then giggles.

"Is it the guy you told me about a while back?"

"Yeah," she mumbles shyly. "Not that he even ever notices me. Doesn't even know my name," she says turning away from me.

"Ah but maybe he will."

"And maybe he won't," she says miserably. She turns her blue eyes towards me and smiles, "But I guess we all have our dreams."

And I remember my dreams.

21

Sometimes I wonder what it'd be like to have a Dad. A normal Dad. A normal family. But it's useless to wonder. It's not a reality so why dream or hope?

Mum's with Dr Alphega while I sit in the waiting room. I watch the children rock on the huge rocking horse. And I notice who goes into the toilets and how long they spend in there. One small girl with long hair and big lips went inside. She's really pretty. She reminds me of Cori.

I check my watch. She's been there for about five minutes now.

Where should I look so as not to draw attention to myself? I wonder what the other people are here for and I wonder what the receptionist thinks of us all.

Mum walks through the door. I don't like it when she comes out. I know they've been talking about me. It's common sense. But they pretend they're not being mean, not discussing me, not intruding.

As I get to my feet the toilet door opens. The big lipped girl appears. I glance at her and we catch each other's eye.

I turn away, embarrassed.

We walk past the usual executive cars and to

our small car.

I know she's been talking about Dad. I can sense it. I guess I'll find out when I next see Dr Alphega.

Tuesday 25th June, Year 9.
Dear Diary,

Again I miss another day from school. I feel useless after therapy. My brain never seems to work. I try to counteract her words so I don't lose my aim. But at the same time I feel a snail creeping into me and I feel strangely reluctant and unable to keep up the fight.

I know this is terrible. It's all my own fault and I WILL fight them all again. But at the moment, with Dad coming back, I hardly have the brainpower to think at all.

And what's more, I know Mum told Dr Alphega about Dad. Can you believe her? Now I don't get the choice about what I say to her. Sometimes I wonder whose doctor she is.

My weight's the same. My stomach doesn't stick out any more, nor any less. The numbers on the scale are the same. It's depressing. But less so than normal. All I want to do at the moment is sleep. I know it's so lazy but I'll get back my fight soon. I promise.

Love,
Jas xxx

I look at the clock and see it's ten minutes past four. School is over with for the day. Everyone will have gone home to homework, television and families. A life that seems so alien to me.

I pick up the phone. I can't help wondering what I've missed at school today. What work did they do? Even if it was boring I'd like to know. I wonder what Cori did today. Did she glide around as the perfect friend to everyone, as usual?

I pick up the upstairs phone and settle comfortably on Mum's bed. I press the numbers and hear the phone connecting to the other end.

"Hi is that you, Beth?"

"Hello You! Where were you today?"

"Oh I didn't feel well after my hospital appointment. Did I miss much?"

"Hmm not much happened really. We had PE and did Javelin which was ok, I guess."

I try to think of the class holding the stick with a huge spear on the end. I've always hated PE and missing this doesn't bother me. But I can imagine Cori holding her stick with such glory.

"Ah you should have seen Cori!" She says as if reading my mind.

"Why? What happened?"

"Oh nothing much. But me and Ade were standing waiting for our turn just behind her. She was being really bitchy about everyone's attempts and how she could do better. But when she threw it," she giggles and gasps for some air. "Oh Jas it was just so funny! She threw it all lopsided. And Ade and I were in hysterics. No one else was laughing and they couldn't understand!"

I start to laugh.

"We were nearly wetting ourselves! And the more no one understood, the more we laughed!"

"I take it when your turn came you showed everyone how brill you were?"

"I wish! We were more useless than Cori. But we didn't care."

The laughing ceases and a short silence takes its place.

162

"So then any gossip your end?" Beth says, shattering the silence.

"Actually I wanted to talk to you about something that's bothering me."

"Sure. Go ahead."

"My dad turned up the other day," I say feeling the tears brimming in my eyes again. I can't believe I'm still crying over it.

"What do you mean? So you mean you do have a Dad then? Oh, I'm so confused."

"Yup, me too." I wonder how I can explain this to her. Where do I begin? Where do I end?

"My dad's just been away all of my life. Not sure where in the world he was. But he wasn't here. Now he's here and he's pretending nothing's happened and wants me in his life. I mean, ugh, how pathetic."

"Oh right. That sounds like a complicated situation to be in."

"Tell me about it. I've refused to speak to him so far! He's just a stranger. I don't want to talk to a selfish stranger."

"Talk about it to that doctor you see."

"Yeah, I spose I could do."

"Is that a yes or a no?"

"It's a maybe."

"Okay. Will you be in school tomorrow?"

"Should be."

"Well we can talk some more tomorrow and maybe we can ask Ade if she's got any advice."

I nod in agreement forgetting she can't see.

"Well, maybe that's what we can talk about in Maths," I say.

"Yeah, cool. We need some distraction from Maths. It's far too boring listening to Sir go on forever and ever and ever."

"I'll see you tomorrow then."

"Sure. Bye," she says.

I put the phone down.

I walk to my bedroom and start to pack my bag for tomorrow's lessons.

I move my diary from my desk to the bed. It makes a gentle dent in the quilt. There are not so many pages left to fill now. I wonder what words will fill them. Will I start a new one when I've finished?

22

I remember my dreams. The dreams of Cori's brown hair and huge lips that form the banana smile. But I don't dream the dreams so vividly.

Did I dream before I had those dreams? I don't remember. I dreamt of being thin when I found my escape from reality. But now the dream stalls and doesn't get past the scales reading six stone. It would be nice to be six stone. That was what the Alien last agreed. I'm nowhere near it.

It's a goal, It says, *we all need goals to work towards. And imagine how you'd feel when you get there!*

As usual It is right. Imagine the feeling...

But I can't imagine it at all.

Beth and Ade are both nattering away in the Maths classroom when I walk in. They see me and grin. It's difficult to remember they're friends and that they want me to sit with them.

I walk over to them

"I was just telling Ade about your dad," Beth says.

I nod.

"Sounds like a real stress," Ade says.

I nod.

I don't know what to say now we are all here. I wonder if I should have said anything at all. Silence creates protection.

"Hm," I say as I look at the textbook with our homework in. "Well, I guess I don't know what to do about it."

"Ok," says Ade leaning back in her chair and raising her eyes. "Let's get this straight. Your Dad came back."

Nod.

"He wants to see you but you don't want to see him."

This is getting boring. How many times do I have to go through this?

"I haven't ever seen him. He left more or less the moment I was born! He's just not a part of my past at all."

"And you don't want to see him because...?"

"Because he left! Why should I want to see someone who abandoned me?" I say it with more feeling than I'd intended. I sounded as if I might care. As if I might be upset. I'm not. I'm not upset at all.

"Where has he been all this time," Beth asks.

I shrug. "You know, I have no idea. Around about. Across the world for all I know. That's the point. He hardly made much effort in trying to stay in touch."

"So this is the first time you heard from him?" she says, thinking.

"Ah, no. I heard from him a few months ago when he sent me some money."

"How much?" they say almost together. Their eyes piercing into me.

I laugh, "Three hundred pounds!"

"No way!" Beth says. "I wish my Dad would

leave cuz then I might get some money."

"Beth!" I say exasperated. "It's not about the money. I didn't take it. I don't want his guilt money."

"But think of all the things you could buy," Ade says. "Think of the good things that can come from it. You could buy so many clothes, CDs and make-up. You'd have so much fun."

"I guess so," I say wondering what it would really be like to go into town knowing I had real money to spend.

"Can't you just see him? Ask him what he's been doing?"

I shrug. I don't want to see him.

"He's a human being you know."

But I'm sure fathers aren't meant to leave and abandon children.

The classroom door opens and in walks the loud, threatening teacher. I look at Beth and she looks at me and then we look at Ade. All three of us groan silently and roll our eyes.

We always hope that he'll be away. Then we'd have a stand in teacher and we wouldn't have to do any work.

He sits at his desk and takes the register.

After he's ticked our names off the list he shouts, "Turn to page thirty-five in your text book and do the questions at the bottom of the page. I don't want to hear ANYONE speaking."

I hear the pages flicking and the silent reading. The pencil cases are opened and pens begin to write. Cori, as always, sits behind me. I feel uncomfortable knowing she is there but I am doing as Dr Alphega suggested and trying to be friendly with Beth and Ade. Somehow that makes me feel better even with Cori sitting behind.

I watch Dr Alphega pick some dust off her skirt and then brush it off her fingers. Will she mention Dad? I know that she knows. I know they've talked about me.

"I think that we need to continue meeting so that we can weaken the Bad Part."

Somehow her words are less intrusive even though I know she's plotting with Mum. Even though I know that the world is against me.

There are no words that I can use. She knows about Cori, she knows about school. She knows more than I'd like her to know.

"Do you agree that the Bad Part makes you feel the need to lose weight?"

I don't know what to say. Her label of the Bad Part seems to be referring to the Alien. The Alien. My friend. It's helped me.

"I know it seems as if this part tells you the truth, but in reality it lies to you." She adds, "Do you think you can see it from my point of view?"

"Possibly," I say trying not to commit myself either way.

"There's something else that we need to talk about today."

My heart beats loudly inside me. Thud. Thud.

"Your mother mentioned that your father has tried to make contact with you. Is that right?"

I nod. I knew that they'd been plotting. It only proves that the Alien knows more than I do and can look after me.

"You must feel very ambiguous about the situation." She looks into the room rather than at me. She mulls the words over and breathes evenly. "Can you tell me anything about your father? I know that you'd told me he was dead."

"I got it wrong," I say jumping in before she can accuse me of lying.

She nods and takes in my words. "Are you able to tell me anything about him?"

"I don't remember him. I've never met him."

"You must feel that he'd abandoned you."

How can she understand that this is what it's like? Has she ever had a father leave her for no real reason?

Why does everyone want to talk about Dad?

Monday 2nd July, Year 9.
Dear Diary,

Life has changed. Food and weight is always there. But now there is the added confusion of Dad. I thought he'd go away. But all anyone wants to do is talk about him. I'm sick of all this talking. What exactly does talking do?

I know what Mum thinks of him. He's not a bad person. He's just a rubbish man at looking after families and drank too much.

But why should I forgive? Why should I go back to someone who may abandon me again? It's like friends. Why have friends when they can hurt you? Why trust anyone?

There seems to be so much happening at the moment that my mind can't take it all in anymore. All my thoughts have turned dull. Dullness and pain amongst the confusion.

I don't know what to do, Diary. Why should I do what everyone wants? I'm old enough to make my own decisions. I'm 14 for goodness sake! They should be treating me like an adult.

Love,
Jas xxx

23

"I think we need to talk," Mum says from behind my closed bedroom door.

"What about?"

"Things."

"I don't want to talk about things."

I hear her settle on the landing. I imagine her sitting there behind my door. And then I go to the closed door and sit in front of it.

No words escape.

"Go on then," I say nastily. I want her to get on with it so that I can get on in peace.

"I really want you to think about seeing Dad."

"No way. How many more times do I have to tell you?"

"Ok then, maybe not meet him. What about speaking to him?"

I don't reply.

"I just think that he is your Dad and he deserves the chance to get to know you." Silence. "Don't you think?"

I hear her shuffling on the floor. I imagine her picking her clear nail varnish off. Pick, pick, picking. And when there's no more nail varnish to pick she will pull the skin around her nails until they're red and sore.

"Jas? What do you think?"

I don't reply.

"I have his number here. You don't need to ring him yet. I just think that it'd be nice if you could think about it. You wouldn't be making any kind of commitment to him. Here's his number." I hear some more shuffling and a small piece of paper appears from under my door.

I pick it up and unravel the tiny paper to reveal a sequence of numbers. Just numbers. The number of a mobile. I wouldn't know it was Dad's number if it weren't for the word, DAD written over it.

"Well, just something to think about," she says. "And one more thing."

"Hmm," I say dubiously.

"I think only a fool would turn down the chance to have three hundred pounds." She laughs. And I can't help laughing too.

I hear her feet walking down the stairs and I get up and put the phone number in my dressing table drawer. The drawer that holds the tablets I still hoard - just in case.

There are usually reasons for things. And anorexia usually has a reason. I wonder what reason I have for being this way? Is it Dad? Cori? Or some unknown tale from my past? Is it important to know?

I manage to muster up a strong enough voice to say something to Dr Alphega.

"Is there a reason for me being like this?"

Being like what? the Alien argues. *There's nothing wrong with you. They just don't want you to be thin. They're all jealous of your will power!*

"What do you mean a reason?"

"Well," I say feeling angry that she can't understand what I'm saying without me having to explain. "Some people have terrible, terrible lives. And you could see how they could get confused and get ill. But I can't see much of a reason for me. Do you think there's something I don't know? Something from my past?"

All these words tumbling from my mouth. Even though they're so quiet I curse myself for saying them. I should not be breaking the rule of silence.

"Sometimes there are reasons that people get ill. Circumstances that prevent people from coping." She pauses. "Everyone has a Bad Part inside them. But not everyone has this part take over to such an extent."

I want to correct her and tell her it's not really taken over, I just know that it'll all be ok if I do what It says.

"I don't think that there are things in your past that you don't remember. I think that there have been a lot of things that you've found difficult to cope with in life and so the Bad Part took a hold of you during these times."

I wonder if she means Cori.

"Like being friends with someone who then breaks the trust that you have in them. It's very damaging."

I don't believe a word of it and I feel all the anger surging through me. "So that's the reason why I'm like this?"

"No. I think that it could have triggered the problems you experience. I don't think it's the cause."

"So what is the cause?"

I want to know. I want the words to all come

out before the Alien starts screaming at me.

"Some people are just prone to these types of difficulties. It's often connected to any insecurities that you experience at a very young age when you should be feeling safe."

I wonder if this could be true.

"And does Dad come into this?"

She doesn't answer immediately. She puts her hand to her face and touches her cheek. And then she says, "I think he is more relevant now because it has enhanced the feelings of abandonment. The Bad Part plays on this to make you believe in it. Like it did when you were friends with Cori."

Somehow it's making some kind of weird sense. There is no real answer but a combination of lots of things.

I wonder if things could change in my head. But the question is too scary to ask.

"I don't have all the answers," she says. "I'm here to help you find them."

The sun suddenly floats in from the window behind. It warms my back and my head.

Maybe it really is possible to feel less alone after all. Maybe.

Wednesday 11th July, Year 9.
Dear Diary,

Do you think it's possible I got it wrong? That really the Alien is not a friend but It's fooling me? I know I want all the mess and confusion in my head to go. But I don't want to give in and let them make me fat. I NEED to lose weight. I MUST lose weight.

Who do I believe? Why is everything so confusing?

I weighed six stone nine pounds this morning and I was so pleased! If I believe them then I will lose the thrill. I will lose myself. Wouldn't I?

Mum gave me Dad's number the other day. She told me to think about ringing him, even though it's a mobile number. Think of the phone bill!

If I phone at least I can get everyone off my back.

I'll talk to Ade and Beth about it at school. See what they say. I know they'll tell me to phone but I still need to ask them anyway.

Oh, nearly forgot! Mum also gave me the money he sent ages ago! I have it here in my room in twenty pound notes, fifteen of them. I've never seen so much money in all my life!

Love,
Jas xxx

24

The early morning sun is warm. It shines through the cracks in the curtains where they're not drawn together properly. The light spreads sequin-like patterns on my pale coloured walls and carpet.

I don't want to get up for school. After lunchtime I have to see Dr Alphega. It's a one off to see her at this unusual time. But it doesn't feel right.

I move the quilt off my legs. It's going to be a hot day. People are already talking about a hot summer. I don't know why they bother. They always forget the hot days as soon as a cold one arrives.

I look at my legs stretching out to the end of the bed. They're still big. Much too big. I can see the fat at the top and the fat just below the knee. The ankles aren't too bad, and the knees are just about ok.

I lift them up one at a time. Holding them in mid air. Counting.

The clock flickers to seven thirty and I hear Mum go into the bathroom.

The day has begun.

Cori never seems to be in the classroom at break times. I stand by the window and silently look down to the field where she's with Ione and their other friends. They sit on the benches and soak up the sun. Always laughing. My eyes are constantly drawn to them, as if something magnetic forces me to them.

Ade walks up to me and touches my arm. "Jas, what you doing?"

"Not a lot," I say, reluctantly diverting my stare from Cori.

Ade walks to the window and looks down to the field. She sees them there, sitting, eating their break and having fun. Then she looks at me.

"Guess the sun always makes people happy."

"Something like that," I say.

She's right, of course. The sun spreads colours in the school that reflect ever onwards and spread throughout. They're brighter than the winter colours and they last longer with fewer clouds in the sky. The lessons are filled with colour, and smiles. Somehow the pressure of work has been temporarily lifted.

"GCSE's are round the corner," Mrs Dorrian says in the English lesson.

It sends a chill down my back. There's still two years to go. Why make time go faster?

Beth looks at me. "Oh no," she whispers. "Here we go. My friend told me that once they start talking about GCSEs you never hear the end of it." She rolls her eyes.

"I'm not sure what the set texts will be for you next year. However, what I do suggest is that you all read as much as possible over the summer."

The class is silent.

"Any reading is always good." Her red hair bouncing as she walks to the blackboard. "I'll just write some books on the board that you should think about reading." The chalk scrapes on the board and leaves white marks.

We scribble down the titles and authors.

"They're excellent books," she says smiling broadly.

Beth rips a piece of paper out of her notebook and then writes something in black ink. She passes it to me.

I tuck the paper under my arm so that Mrs Dorrian can't see our communication. *This is our last summer before GCSEs let's NOT do ANY of her reading!* The note ends with a face that winks up at me.

I look over at her but she's pretending not to notice. So I write back: *Who needs Shakespeare? Not us! Yeah, let's have fun in the holidays. Our last chance of freedom!!*

I push the note back. Beth reads it and whispers, "You'll not be free until you stop your dieting."

I feel her words slice into me. What right does she have to ruin our communication with words like that? What does she know anyway?

Mrs Dorrian stops writing and faces the class. "Although I don't know exactly which texts you will be studying next year, I know that I won't be teaching some of you. English will work differently in September and you will be put into sets. I will be taking set one." She puts her list of authors onto her desk. And then she sits down, waiting for us to finish, and waiting for the bell to go.

The bell rings loudly. More loudly than usual, it seems.

"See ya, Beth," I say as I walk out of the English room.

"Where you going?"

"My appointment."

"Oh yeah. Forgot."

"Say bye to Ade for me and see you guys tomorrow."

"Ok. Have fun!"

"As if!"

I run down the steps two at a time hoping to get to the glass door of the school before all the crowds start dribbling out of the classrooms.

My feet echo on the fragile tiles. The noise loud and yet insignificant in the midst of so many other noises.

I push the glass doors and enter into the sunlit day. The sun pouring gold onto everything.

Outside everyone looks like glowing angels.

Warings looks somewhat dull and dark compared to the glowing angels at school. I walk up the usual corridors with Dr Alphega at the unusual time. I can smell burnt toast escaping from one of the downstairs rooms.

One of the receptionists had walked in with a bag from the supermarket. French bread was sticking through the top of the plastic bag.

All anyone thinks about is food, the Alien says.

When I sit down in the room I notice the maroon seats are warm with sun. And then it hits me. Where are my sunglasses? I don't have them with me.

Idiot! It says. *You have to sit here for twenty*

minutes without sunglasses. She'll be able to see through you and know EVERYTHING. You'll never survive. It'll be hell forever more.

Dr Alphega sits in her thoughtful position as my heart beats and pounds inside. What will she say? What will I do?

"I'm glad you could make it today. I know that's it's a different time to meet." She pauses. "It must feel strange. But it won't happen very often. I just couldn't get in for our normal appointment time this morning."

Nothing's changed. The Alien was wrong. I don't need the sunglasses.

"Jas!" Mum shouts up the stairs.

I reluctantly open my bedroom door. "What?" I say harshly, annoyed for being distracted from my thoughts.

"Someone here for you."

I walk down the stairs. I don't know who it is and I don't care. I want whoever it is to go so that I can get on with what I'm doing.

"Hello Jasmine," a man says.

I look at him. He stands tall in the doorway and strangely familiar. A balding man with a dark beard that is speckled with white strands.

"Dad," I say without feeling.

My heart is slow. Is it still beating? Am I still here? Alive? Living?

"Oh," I say suddenly jumping into my mind and remembering, "You ought to have your money back. Thanks but no thanks."

He shakes his head. "It's for you. Surely a pretty girl like you can think of plenty of things to spend money on." He laughs. "All girls are short of money!"

He has a point.

Now we're here, standing in front of each other, I don't know what to say. This was why I didn't want to see him.

"I just wondered, Jas," he says tentatively, "if, maybe we could meet up at some point?"

"Well," I say scrunching my face up and looking up at the ceiling.

"I know it's really hard for you and everything. No pressure. It'd just be nice to catch up. It's been a long time."

I don't say anything.

"It's been a too long."

I nod. "Yes, all my life is a long time."

"I know. I'm sorry. Things just get ... Well, none of that's important now. I just want the chance to know you."

"Maybe," I say.

I hear Mum's shoes on the wooden floor in the hall.

"You could ring him couldn't you, Jas?"

I nod.

"After all, we'd really rather you didn't normally turn up unannounced like this."

"Oh I know!" he says hurriedly. "I just started worrying in case you'd lost my number."

He takes his pen out of his jacket pocket and writes something down fast. Then he hands it to me.

I nervously step towards him and take it from him. His phone number is on the paper.

I feel bad.

"Yeah, I'll ring you soon and let you know."

Mum says, "Maybe just phoning would be good for now."

"Whichever is easiest," he says eagerly. "Well,

I'll be off now. Don't forget to have fun with the money and speak to you soon."

He hurries up the path and I close the front door.

25

Monday 16th July, Year 9.
Dear Diary,
  July is the month of hot weather and sunny days. We've already had quite a few hot days this month. I've learnt to hate the sun. The sun is when people are happy and laugh. I see Cori outside with Ione all the time. They always laugh. Always happy.

  I hear laughing people walk past my bedroom window. I see their smiles without even having to see their faces.

  Happy people remind me of how distant I am from everyone in the world. I am trying to be like them, but I know I'm still different.

  School is breaking-up in a couple of days. We'll get our reports. I'm dreading mine. We already know the sets we'll be in next year and I'm in set 1 for English! Can you believe that? I'm actually good at something other than taking photographs! And I've also got Mrs Dorian again which is really good because I don't like the other English teachers. Guess what? Cori isn't even in Set 1 which is a first for her.

  And then there's Dad...

I sit with my pen in my hand. What is there to write about him?

I don't wear my sunglasses to stare out into a darkened world anymore. I have discovered I don't need them. I don't even seem to mind the fragments of light breaking up the dullness at Warings hospital.

I don't know how to speak. I don't know how to say words. My mind is a tangled mess.

Dr Alphega says, "I've been thinking about school and how you're breaking up today. I've been wondering how it is for you." Pause. "Your descriptions of Garret Bell being made up of glass and echoing words has stayed in my mind."

"The echo glass," I say suddenly.

"Pardon?"

I turn to her slightly. "The echo glass. A glass school that echoes words."

"Yes, that's a nice phrase and it clearly describes what's been happening. These words you hear in that place hurt you so much. The words that Cori used last year keep bouncing back."

I nod.

"But in reality the school does not hold those cruel words. The school is where people go and learn."

I'm silent. What does she mean? If they're not in the school where are the words?

"Do you agree with that?" she asks.

Suddenly it hits me. "The words are in me?" I say quietly, tentatively. Surely this is wrong to be saying so much?

"I think the words could well be in you. And they're echoing back again and again. The Bad

Part feeds off those words and gets stronger."

"But I don't do it by choice," I say trying to defend myself. "It's just the Alien."

"Of course you don't do it by choice."

Another silence. A different silence.

"You mean," I say hesitating slightly, "I'm the one who's the ..." I can barely put the words together. My voice drops to a whisper. I know I have to say it, "I'm the echo glass?"

She smiles slightly and says, "You know, I think you are. The Bad Part, or what you have called the alien, took over when there were terrible things happening around you. It felt safe for you to listen to those echoes. But in the end this part bullies you as much as Corisande did."

I've said the words. But I don't like it.

"Glass is fragile. When the glass is broken the echoes will stop. And I am here to weaken that bad part. To make the good strong again. Those words that you hear inside all the time, that's not the real you. The alien just wants you to believe them so that it can undermine you."

Perhaps it makes some sense. The Alien is happiest when It hears Cori's words.

"Would you be able to keep your weight the same for me?"

Six stone six pounds is so close to my goal. "I don't know."

"If you could manage to stop losing weight and just try to keep it the same then you would be giving less power to the Bad Part."

Less power to the Bad Part. That would be less power to the Alien.

If I did agree I'd be under less pressure to lose weight. It wouldn't have to be my fault anymore. There would be someone I could blame. Dr

Alphega would be to blame for not allowing me to lose weight.

"Ok, I'll try," I say quietly.

I leave the room feeling strange.

The grass is dry under the midday sun. The benches are cluttered with girls in navy uniforms.

"Hi, Ade," I say smiling.

I see Cori sitting with Ione on a bench not too far from us. They both look at me and giggle with each other.

"Beth's coming," Ade says.

I see her walking towards us. She is smiling her delicate smile under the sun.

"Hiya, Jas," she says. She's holding a bottle of coke in one hand and an essay in the other.

"Look what I got from Mrs Dorrian."

I look at the front of the essay. She has an A.

"Wow, that's really good," I say.

We all smile.

"Have fun at your appointment this morning?"

"Yeah, course," I say pulling a face at her. She'd never understand how it really worked. There would be no point in ever trying to explain.

"Listen," I say, "Dad turned up AGAIN. I spoke to him this time. Told him I would phone him. Do you think I should? I don't know if I will meet him but if things went ok, which, I spose they might, I could meet him one day soon."

They both watch as I explain to them. Their eyes burning into me and putting me off.

"Not that he's forgiven or anything," I add.

They laugh.

"Well, it's true!"

"Yeah I think you should phone him. You told

185

him you would," Beth says.

Ade smiles too. "Shall we all meet up in the holidays too? We could go shopping or go to the cinema. Ha! Offer *her*," she says winking at me, "some moral support!"

"Yeah! How fab would that be?" Beth says.

I smile. "That would be good," I say. I think of the money that Dad won't take back. Maybe I could spend some of it. "I've got the money Dad gave me. So I guess I could afford to go shopping."

"Oh, it's all right for some!"

"Actually I was kinda thinking I would buy a better camera. You know, a digital one with a zoom lens. What do you think?"

"Definitely! You're going to be such a brill photographer. And you'll deff get an A in your Photography GCSE! Well and your English one come to that!" Beth says.

Ade nods in agreement. I feel a smile stretching across my face.

"You have chosen to do Photography next year haven't you?" Ade says.

"Of course," I say, "I'm not stupid, ya know!"

I remember that I have my camera with me in my bag. "Hey, can I take your pics?"

"Sure" Ade says smiling.

I jump up and stand a little way from them. They move closer and put their arms around each other, smiling their smiles to the camera.

Click. The camera winds itself on. The sun is shining down on us making it the perfect day for taking pictures.

I sit back down between them. Beth passes Ade her coke while she reads the comments on her essay.

I look around the vast field. It feels as if Cori's still nearby although she seems strangely distant. I turn around to where she's sitting to see if she's looking at me. And there she is, her face looking confused with her eyebrows knotted. Her angel glow is gone and her serenity has evaporated. Why does she look at me with that puzzled expression?

It must be because I have friends. True friends. And we both know that we won't ever speak again. Her words, her image, they may fool other people but they don't get to me anymore.

I am the echo glass.

Fragile glass cracks and breaks. I'll smash the glass inside me so that the hateful words will stop echoing...

The electric bell rings shrilly shattering my thoughts. And the echo glass collapses to shards, cutting through the image of Cori's beauty and the hateful words that exist inside me.

I was the Echo Glass.

Acknowledgements

I would like to thank Gina Standring for all her hard work and willingness to read and criticize my work with an objective eye.

I would also like to thank my Mum who has promised to never read this book. And also to Alex who has helped to let people know about my book.